WEEKLY READER
Children's Book Club
Education Center • Columbus 16, Ohio

PRESENTS

The Pink Motel

by Carol Ryrie Brink

Illustrated by Sheila Greenwald
The Macmillan Company · New York · 1959

The Pink Motel
by Carol Ryrie Brink

WEEKLY READER
Children's Book Club
Edition, 1960

Library of Congress catalog card number: 59-12838

First Printing

The Macmillan Company, New York
Brett-Macmillan Ltd., Galt, Ontario

Printed in the United States of America
American Book-Stratford Press, Inc., N. Y.

For David Owen Brink and
Clark Howard Hunter with love

Contents

1. Six Weather Vanes for Seven Houses

Until Kirby Mellen was ten nothing very exciting had ever happened to him or his father or his mother or his little sister Bitsy. The Mellens did not know any unusual people, and they did not do any unusual things. Of course, Kirby always hoped that something exciting might happen. To be prepared for anything, Kirby wore on his left breast the J. Edgar Hoover Junior G-Man badge which had come in a package of Krispy-Krackles. But he had never had to use it.

Then suddenly Kirby's mother inherited a motel, and things did begin to happen. The motel came to Mrs. Mellen from her great-granduncle Hiram Stonecrop. Mrs. Mellen had not seen her Uncle Hiram since she was the age of Kirby, and she was pretty nearly flabbergasted when she heard that the poor old gentleman had died and left her a motel.

I

"Uncle Hiram was a very interesting man," she said, "and I remember now that he used to tell me he was going to leave me something valuable when he died. But I certainly never expected a motel."

"What is a motel?" asked Bitsy. Bitsy was a year younger than Kirby and she liked to ask questions without taking time to listen to the answers. "Why? What? and Where?" asked Bitsy, and then dashed away to ask something different of somebody else. This time, however, she was so interested that she stayed and waited for the answer.

"I know," Kirby said. "A motel is a kind of hotel, only there aren't any elevators."

"Six units," read Mr. Mellen out of the letter that had come from Uncle Hiram's lawyer. "That's not very large. Six little houses, I suppose, all in a row, and in Florida of all places."

"Why 'of all places'?" asked Bitsy.

"Because Florida is so far away," said Mr. Mellen.

"And we have never been there," said Kirby.

"Dear me!" said Kirby's mother. "What shall we do about it?"

2

"We'll have to go down and run it, of course," said Kirby's father. "Until we can sell it, that is."

There was only one person in the family who could tell them anything about the motel, and that was second cousin Rose Thornapple.

"Yes, I visited Uncle Hiram there once," she said, "and it is a very peculiar place."

"*Peculiar?*" asked Mrs. Mellen nervously. She was always suspicious of anything peculiar.

"It's pink," said Cousin Rose. "Not white or brown or gray, like an ordinary motel. It's a real bright pink, a speaking pink, as you might say. And, whether because of the color or because Uncle Hiram was a rather unusual person, it attracted the most unusual guests."

"What do you mean *unusual?*" asked Mr. Mellen, also rather nervously, for he was always suspicious of anything unusual.

"I don't know exactly," said Cousin Rose. "It's nothing you can put your finger on, but I felt it as soon as I set foot down there. The place was peculiar. The guests were very strange."

"Tsk! tsk! tsk!" said Kirby's mother. But Kirby was pleased. For some reason he had always liked peculiar and unusual things. A pink motel and most unusual guests! He thought it might be fun.

The inheritance was really like a Christmas present, for it arrived just before the beginning of Christmas vacation.

"Let me see," said Kirby's father. "The children will have three weeks' vacation. We'll just about have time to fly down to Florida, put the motel in running order, and sell it before time for the children to go back to school."

Mrs. Mellen began to get their summer clothes out of the closets; for, although there was snow on the ground in Minnesota, she firmly believed that the weather would be warm in Florida.

After he had heard the news Kirby went up to his room and began to pack the things that seemed most necessary to him. Of course, he packed his space helmet and his chemistry set and his model airplane kit. He looked at the various guns and pistols which he had not used much lately. When he was five years old, he had learned from watching television how to be the quickest on the draw of any boy in the neighborhood. But now he was more interested in the idea of being the first boy to visit the moon in a space ship.

However, he decided to take his two best pistols, the ones in the imitation leather holster that were easiest to draw quickly. He also polished up his J. Edgar Hoover Junior G-Man badge so that it shone like real silver.

Hanging at the back of his closet was a bright pink necktie which Kirby could not remember having seen before. He took it out and tried it on. It was a very bright pink, and Kirby was pleased with his appearance.

As he was admiring himself in the mirror, Bitsy appeared, wearing a bright pink hair ribbon.

"Look what I found at the back of my closet," she said.

Mrs. Mellen was surprised when she saw the children. "For goodness sake! where did you children find those

4

terribly pink old things? I thought they had disappeared long ago."

"We found them in the backs of our closets, Mama," said Kirby.

"Where did they come from?" asked Bitsy.

"Dear me!" said Mrs. Mellen, "your great-great-granduncle Hiram must have sent them to you when you were babies. No one but Uncle Hiram would have sent anything so pink. Better take them off now. They look most unusual."

"Oh, Mama, please let us wear them," begged Bitsy, and Kirby said, "They'll match the pink motel."

"All right," Mrs. Mellen said. "But don't be annoyed if people stare."

"We won't," the children said. Something about the pink necktie and the pink hair ribbon made Kirby and Bitsy feel very happy and gay. Kirby whistled as he packed, and Bitsy sang.

The way Bitsy packed was to toss doll clothes, paper dolls, crayons and small stuffed animals higgledy-piggledy into a suitcase with her pajamas and toothbrush crammed in on top. Naturally Kirby was much neater than that, and he had a tube of toothpaste, too.

In a very short time the Mellen family was ready to fly to Florida. Their flight to the South was like a trick of magic. They got onto the plane in snowsuits and overshoes, and stepped out of it in shorts and summer dresses. This was the first strange thing.

Mr. Mellen hired a taxi to take them from the airport out into the country to the motel, and all along the way were large red and yellow and purple flowers, like the flowers a magician pulls out of his hat. That was the second strange thing. To a Minnesota family in December, this was quite fantastic.

Although they had been warned in advance, the Mellens were also astonished by the color of the motel. As Cousin Rose had said, it was a "speaking pink." It was pinker than Kirby's necktie or Bitsy's hair ribbon. It was pink, *pink*, PINK. On the small square of lawn in front of the motel two life-sized plaster flamingos were standing, and they were pink, too.

"Well!" said Kirby and Bitsy, and Mr. and Mrs. Mellen said, "Well, well, well!"

They had expected six little pink houses, but there were really seven. The one in the middle was larger than the other six, and it was marked OFFICE.

Behind the seven pink houses (and perhaps that is partly why they looked so pink) was the sea. It was dazzlingly blue except where the waves broke in white foam on the yel-

6

low sand. The colors were brighter than anything Kirby or Bitsy had ever seen in the North. It was like a picture they might make with their crayons, bright pink, bright blue, bright yellow and white.

"Dear me!" said Kirby's mother, "it's quite pretty, isn't it?"

"I hear it," Bitsy said. "What is it saying?"

Kirby was already listening to the sounds and trying to figure them out. There was the steady *whoosh, whoosh* sound of the waves coming up on the shore, and there was a dry, rattling sound of wind among palm leaves. Looking about, Kirby saw that each pink cottage had a tall coconut palm tree standing guard over it. The palm leaves were long and stiff, and, moving against one another, they made the rattling sound.

But there was still another sound which puzzled him for a moment, until he discovered that each one of the six smaller cottages had a weather vane on top. Only the office in the center had no weather vane. Although the six little houses were exactly alike in size, shape and color, each one had a different kind of weather vane. Someone had carved the weather vanes very carefully into strange and delightful shapes. One was like a flying duck; another was like a crowing cock. One was a prancing horse; another was an airplane. One was a leaping dolphin; another had two little men sawing wood.

When the wind came in from the sea, all of the weather vanes turned and flapped and sawed and flew and pranced like mad. They made a wonderful whirring, banging,

7

buzzing and whistling sound. The palm leaves rattled, the waves roared, and the various and sundry weather vanes, like the various and sundry instruments in an orchestra, each played its own particular tune.

"Dear me!" said Kirby's mother again, as she put her hands over her ears. "What a racket!"

But Kirby and Bitsy jumped up and down and waved their arms like the arms of the weather vanes. The sounds seemed to them to be exciting as well as pleasant. As if there were not noise enough already, they both began to shout, "Hooray!"

They now noticed that the office had another sign on the door which said CLOSED. There was sand on the door-sill and dust on the windowpanes. It was apparent that no one had occupied the Pink Motel since Uncle Hiram had left it.

Mr. Mellen took a key out of his pocket and fitted it into the office door.

"This is the owner's house," he said. "This is where we shall live—that is, of course, until we can sell the place and return to our home in the North."

"Shall we take the CLOSED sign down?" asked Kirby.

"Not yet," replied his father. "First of all we must clean the place up, and get ready for guests."

The front door opened onto a narrow hall which led back to the family living quarters. On the left side of the hall was a tiny office nearly filled by a large roll-top desk and a swivel chair.

Kirby's mother took one look into the office and threw

up her hands in horror. "What a mess!" she said. "I hope the rest of the place isn't as bad as this."

The office really did look untidy, but pleasantly so. It was the kind of mess that a pack rat or a crow might make by bringing all sorts of treasures into his nest. Kirby's fingers itched to get into it.

But Mr. Mellen said, "I expect this was Uncle Hiram's special corner. We'll have to sort it out and clean it up, of course. But, for the time being, we had better close it, and spend our time in putting the rest of the place into running order. We can examine Uncle Hiram's private papers later when we have more time."

Mrs. Mellen was already looking into the kitchen.

"It's a man's kitchen," she said, "but I guess I can make do." Remembering what Cousin Rose had said about the place, she added disapprovingly, "*Unusual*, is it? *Dirty*, I call it, and untidy, too. But that we can soon fix."

She began to fly around with dustpan and mop, while Mr. Mellen took hammer and nails and mended broken doorsteps and loose shutters.

Kirby and Bitsy ran right down to the sea and took off their shoes and stockings. The sand was hard and clean, and little waves kept coming up to play tag with their feet. One of the coco palm trees shook itself and dropped a coconut right at Kirby's feet.

"Well!" said Kirby, "that's a nice beginning."

"I hope we stay," said Bitsy.

2. A Messy Desk

There was so much to do at the Pink Motel that Kirby and even Bitsy were kept busy. First the cottages had to be opened to the breeze; then the bedding needed airing, and all of the sheets and towels needed washing. Mr. Mellen strung a very long clothesline between the seven palm trees, and soon dozens of white sheets and pillowcases and towels danced and flapped in the sunshine. They added popping and snapping noises to the orchestra of weather vanes and palms and sea.

"As soon as we can afford it," Mr. Mellen said, "we must paint the motel white or brown or gray, so that it will appeal to ordinary people."

"We certainly must," agreed his wife. "It is far too pink."

But Kirby couldn't help thinking that the bright pink houses made a very pretty picture against the blue sea and

sky with the rows of clean white sheets flap-flapping between the palm trees.

Apparently he was not the only one who thought so.
Before noon the next day, an odd-looking old car drove
up to the motel, and an old lady hopped out. She was thin
and brown but she had a brush of curly white hair all over
her head.

"Hi!" she said to Kirby.

"Hi!" said Kirby, "but we aren't open for business yet,
ma'am."

"That's all right," the lady said. "I don't mind at all if
things are in a mess. I relish a proper mess, and I really
must stop and paint you."

"Paint us?" cried Kirby in alarm. He thought that she
meant to cover the beautiful pink with white or gray or
brown, just as his father meant to do someday. "I like it
pink," he said. "I like it just the way it is."

"Why, so do I!" the lady said. "You didn't think I
meant to change it, did you? This is my favorite place.
Tell your folks I'll take cottage number one, the Duck,
and I'll pay by the week, as usual. Now I must get started
while the light's just right."

From the back of her car, the old lady began to unload
easels and canvas and paints and brushes. Kirby saw with
surprise that she was planning to paint a picture of the
Pink Motel, sheets, towels, coco palms and all. He stood
there staring with his mouth wide open, until the old lady
called, "Run along now. Didn't I ask you to tell your
folks I was here? The way you're staring at me, I might

be a blue-faced monkey with a purple tail instead of a nice old lady minding her own business."

"Excuse me," Kirby said, "I didn't mean to stare, but—"

"I don't like buts," the lady said. "They have sharp corners."

"I don't know why—" began Kirby.

"Go! Go! Go!" cried the lady. "Argufying, amplifying and debate are things I can't abide."

At that Kirby picked up his feet and went fast. He ran to tell his mother that the first strange guest had arrived.

"Oh, for goodness sake!" said Mrs. Mellen. "I wasn't ready yet. What shall I do?"

"We'll help you, Mama," Bitsy and Kirby said. "And, Mama, she says she doesn't mind a mess," Kirby added.

"She'll find no mess in *my* motel," said Kirby's mother. "Come along now."

So they all rushed around, and before long the floor was swept, the bed was made, and everything was as neat as a pin in cottage number one, the Duck.

When everything was ready, Kirby went out to tell the lady that she could stay. He stood behind her and looked at her picture, and he was very much surprised. It had pink in it, and blue and white, and a little green and brown and yellow, but it didn't look like anything except squares and triangles and wiggly lines.

"I can do better than that," said Kirby, before he remembered to mind his manners.

"I dare say you can," replied the old lady calmly. She seemed better tempered now that she was painting. She added kindly, "I used to do better than this myself, but folks won't buy a simple picture of houses and sheets and trees any more. I have to live, and the folks who buy pictures enjoy their eggs scrambled these days. However, if you're going to brag, you'd better let me see what *you* can do."

Kirby liked to draw, so he took a stick and drew in the sand seven small houses and two trees with a sheet.

"Of course there are more trees and sheets, and I haven't any pink," said Kirby, "but this is the way *I* would do it, if *I* made a picture."

"It will do for a start," said the lady, "if you don't get uppity about it. As soon as an artist gets uppity, he is likely to find himself downity. But who *are* you? I expected to see Hiram Stonecrop."

"Great-great-granduncle Hiram died," said Kirby. "I am Kirby Mellen."

"Died, you say? Hiram Stonecrop died? Oh, I'm very sorry! Such an unusual man, your uncle Hiram. I shall miss him greatly. He was an old, old friend." She paused a moment to wipe away a tear, then added more cheerfully, "And you don't know me, do you? I'm Miss Elizabeth Ferry."

" 'Lizabeth is my name, too," said Bitsy, who had come up to stand beside Kirby.

"Then blessings on you!" said Miss Ferry. "It's a very good name, and I hope it will be of use to you for as many hundreds of years as I have used it."

"Hundreds?" cried the children in surprise.

"Can't you take a joke?" laughed Miss Ferry. Then she added, "Well, it's time to knock off for lunch now. Would you care to join me?"

"Well, I don't know if Mama would let us," began Kirby.

"Ask her! Ask her!" commanded Miss Ferry. "I like to do things suddenly."

Kirby and Bitsy both ran fast to ask, but Mother said, "Certainly not! Our first guest? You mustn't make a nuisance of yourselves."

14

So the children had to tell Miss Ferry that they were very sorry but they would be unable to accept.

"It's just as well," Miss Ferry said. "Perhaps there wouldn't have been enough."

But Kirby thought there would have been, for he couldn't help seeing what an amazing array of sandwiches, tarts and small, unexplained tidbits Miss Ferry suddenly produced out of a hamper. He was the more surprised because he had not even noticed the hamper before.

Reluctantly Kirby and Bitsy went into the central house, and ate a good, plain vegetable soup which is always very nutritious and healthful for young people. Mrs. Mellen was rapidly turning Uncle Hiram's man-kitchen into a lady-kitchen where proper food was properly prepared.

After lunch Miss Ferry came to the office to sign up for her cottage.

"I am certainly sorry to hear about Hiram," she said. "Still he was very, very old, and I expect his time had come. But I had always hoped that he would share his secret with me before he died."

"*Secret?*" asked Mrs. Mellen nervously. She was always suspicious of secrets.

"Yes," said Miss Ferry. "He had one, you know. Perhaps he left it to you?"

"No," Kirby's mother said. "He left us the motel, but so far as I know, that is all. Do you have any idea what kind of a secret it was?"

"No, I don't," said Miss Ferry. "That's one of the

things that has kept me coming back here year after year. I always wanted to find out."

"But maybe there wasn't any secret," Kirby's father said.

"Oh, I think there was," said Miss Ferry. "Hiram couldn't have been as happy and pleased with himself as he always was, unless he had a secret. Some people thought it was money that he had hidden. You know the early Spanish explorers came along this coast—pirates, too. Some folks thought Hiram had found buried treasure. But I always believed that his secret was something important that he had learned. He had lived a long time, and I think he had discovered some secret recipe for being happy. If he didn't leave it to you, I suppose that we shall never know what it was."

"There is a terrible clutter of papers and scraps of this and that in his old roll-top desk," said Kirby's father. "I haven't had time to look into it yet. It will take months to sort it over, and for the present I am leaving it as it is."

"Well, if you find anything interesting there that you care to share," said Miss Ferry, "I'd be very glad to add it to my collection. And now, to change the subject, has Mr. Carver arrived yet?"

"No," said Kirby's mother, "you are the first one. Is Mr. Carver someone we ought to know?"

"He comes every year," said Miss Ferry. "He's the one who whittles out the weather vanes, and I'm sure he'll be back because there's one weather vane still missing. He wouldn't like to leave the place unfinished."

16

"It's the one over our house, the one in the center," Kirby said. "I noticed right away. Do you think Mr. Carver will come someday and make us one?"

Miss Ferry rubbed the side of her nose in an odd little way she had.

"I'm sure he will," she said. "Mr. Carver believed that Hiram had a secret, too, and that was why he left Hiram's weather vane until last. Most workmen would begin with the proprietor's house, but Mr. Carver kept hoping to discover Hiram's secret, so that he would be able to carve something suitable for his roof. Now that you are here, I suspect he will study *you* and make a weather vane which suits *your* family."

This seemed an excellent idea to Bitsy and Kirby.

"We shan't be here long," said Mr. Mellen. "As soon as we get the place cleaned up and running smoothly, we shall paint it a proper color and sell it to someone else. Mr. Carver had better wait until the new owner comes, before he designs the last weather vane."

Kirby and Bitsy and Miss Ferry all looked very sober when Mr. Mellen said this. "Oh, Daddy!" Kirby said.

"It's a nice place," Miss Ferry said. "It would be too bad to give it up too hastily, and as to the color—"

"You see my husband has a regular office in the North," explained Kirby's mother. "We've never tried to run a motel before. It's all new to us, and the children's vacation will soon be over and we'll have to get back so that they will not miss anything."

"Mama, we haven't missed anything yet," said Kirby.

17

"I understand how it is," said Miss Ferry. "Well, good luck to you." She took her key and went away to cottage number one, the Duck. Kirby looked after her for a moment. There was something very likable about her, and at the same time she did seem rather strange.

"Kirby," Mr. Mellen said, "I haven't time to go through Uncle Hiram's desk now, but will you just poke around in it and see if you can find a guest book or register? It would be useful to know who the regular customers are. This Miss Ferry now, and this Mr. Carver—perhaps there are other regular guests whom we should be expecting."

"All right, Daddy," Kirby said.

"Don't destroy anything, Kirby," Mr. Mellen said. "Just look for a guest book of some kind."

Kirby went obediently into the little cubbyhole which had been Great-great-granduncle Hiram's office. No one had made any attempt to tidy it. The roll-top desk was bulging with papers and shells and old books and fishing reels, and many other things. Nothing seemed to be valu-

18

able. A shelf ran around the wall, and on it were a great many coconut shells which were also stuffed with string and fishhooks and small pieces of paper. The bits of paper were of many colors, but most of them were pink. Kirby suspected that the coconut shells, like the filing cabinet in his father's office up north, kept Uncle Hiram's business secrets and personal treasures. The only difference was that Father's filing cabinet was so neat that it was quite uninteresting, whereas Uncle Hiram's coconut shells were full of mystery and promise.

Kirby noticed that some of the coconut shells had labels on them, but, although Kirby could read very well, he couldn't make head nor tail of the labels. *"Hap. I,"* *"Wint. 02,"* *"Un. Imp. Bus."* What could a person possibly make out of labels like those?

Kirby took one of the loose bits of paper from the desk. It was a blue one, and he soon saw that it was a receipt for a pint of pink paint bought in the year 1928. He took up a piece of pink paper which had been folded neatly into a triangle. Inside the pink paper were written the words,

A Place for Everything and Everything in its Place

"Dear me!" Kirby said to himself. "Uncle Hiram didn't take that bit of advice very seriously." He opened another slip of pink paper and read the words,

Be Yourself

"Well," said Kirby to himself, "what else could I be?" Beneath many papers, Kirby finally found the motel guest book. To make sure that this was what he wanted, he opened it and looked inside. Yes, here were the names of all of the guests who had stayed at the Pink Motel. The record went back many years, and, instead of HOTEL REGISTER, on the first page, Uncle Hiram had written, HIRAM STONECROP'S FRIENDS.

I like that, thought Kirby. Glancing through the list of names, he saw

Miss Elizabeth Ferry—occupation, artist
address, Greenwich Village, New York
(always pays promptly)
Mr. Jonathan Carver—occupation, uncertain
address, unknown
(he will pay for his room in odd jobs)

There were other names which intrigued Kirby, but the one which interested him most was

The Great Marvello—occupation, magician
address, the World
(if he does not have the money,
he will pick it out of thin air)

"Hmm!" said Kirby thoughtfully. He was something of an amateur magician himself, and he certainly hoped that Marvello would come to stay at the Pink Motel before he and Bitsy had to go north to school.

Kirby put the papers carefully back on the desk, took the guest book and went away, closing the door behind him.

"Daddy, here is the book," said Kirby.

20

"Thank you, Kirby," Mr. Mellen said. "I'm glad that someone can find something in that untidy office. Perhaps I shall have to put you in charge of finding things in Uncle Hiram's office."

"Good," Kirby said. "I think I'd like that."

Outside Kirby met Bitsy.

"What shall we do now?" asked Bitsy.

"Let's take a dip," said Kirby, "and then let's go up the road and see if we can see Mr. Carver coming."

So, after their dip, they went up the road, and they looked and looked; but sunset came and no Mr. Carver. The only person who came down the road was a little colored boy named Big.

"Why is your name Big?" asked Kirby. "You aren't as big as I am. I'm ten. How old are you?"

"Ten," said Big.

"Then you are really little," Kirby said.

"I am bigger than all my brothers and sisters," said the new boy. "Mr. Stonecrop, he always called me Big. He said that was a mighty good name for me because I can do a lot of work for my size."

"What kind of work?"

"Run errands, carry bags, fetch ice water, sweep the sand off the doorstep."

"That's what I'm going to do," said Kirby.

"Maybe I help you," said Big. He smiled a very large and pleasant smile, and Kirby and Bitsy knew that they would like him.

3. The Problem
of the Coconuts

It was Big who showed them how to open coconuts.

"Let's have a coconut for breakfast," Kirby said early one morning.

"All right. Let's do," said Bitsy. Big had not come over yet, and in any case they would not have thought to ask him for help.

It was the third morning of their stay at the Pink Motel, and they had not had time to eat a coconut, although the obliging trees had been dropping them down all around. Kirby had made a neat pile of fallen nuts behind the central cabin, and now he and Bitsy ran out and selected a large one.

"Now children, be careful not to overeat," said Kirby's mother. Then she hurried away, because she had a busy day ahead of her.

"We'll try not to, Mama," called Kirby.

He held the coconut up and shook it, and he could hear the milk sloshing around inside.

"Mmm!" said Kirby with anticipation.

"Where do you start?" asked Bitsy.

"Well," said Kirby, "I guess we start by peeling off the shell."

"Yes," Bitsy said, "but how?" Bitsy believed that Kirby could do anything, and now she expected him to take the shell right off the coconut and let her begin to eat it.

The coconut was smooth and hard, and there wasn't a crack or a dent anywhere. Kirby could not tell where to begin. First he dropped it on the ground, but it bounced back, as round and hard as ever. Next he tried banging two nuts together, with no better luck.

The harder Kirby tried to crack the coconut, the hungrier he got. Breakfast is a meal that you like to eat promptly, but this went on and on. Finally Kirby said to Bitsy, "We had better eat our Krispy-Krackles. We can still have the coconut for lunch."

"All right," Bitsy said, "I'll eat my Krispy-Krackles. But remember, you promised to crack the coconut for lunch."

After breakfast Kirby started in on the coconut again. This time he took a hammer from the tool shed and hit the coconut hard. The hammer made a little dent in the shell, but nothing else happened.

"You didn't hit it hard enough," said Bitsy.

Bang! bang! bang! went Kirby's hammer. The coconut bounced up and came down on Kirby's toe.

"Ouch!" said Kirby. "You're a fine one, you are, you horrible old coconut, you!"

"Tut-tut!" said a voice behind him. "It won't do you a bit of good to get mad. What you need is a chisel."

Kirby looked around and saw Miss Elizabeth Ferry, the artist. She was wearing a beautifully paint-spotted pair of overalls and a green eyeshade.

"Run get your father's chisel," she said. "I'll show you how to do it in a jiffy."

So Kirby fetched the chisel.

"It's as easy as pie," Miss Ferry said. She placed the chisel against the side of the coconut, and hit it smartly with the hammer. Up shot the coconut, like a thing possessed, and knocked off Miss Ferry's green eyeshade.

"They *are* quite a nuisance to get into," she said. "Sometimes I wonder why people bother. Do you really like coconuts anyway?"

"I think so," Kirby said. "We've never had one. That's why we wanted to find out."

"In that case, it's important," Miss Ferry said, banging away with hammer and chisel. "Too bad I didn't bring my wand," she added. "One seldom needs a wand nowadays, with all the electric buttons to push. I probably left it in the broom closet in my apartment. It would have made all this much easier, however."

"You have a wand?" asked Kirby in astonishment.

"My goodness!" laughed Miss Ferry. "Can't you take a joke?"

While they were all talking and laughing and banging

24

at the coconut, Big came up and stood watching them with his hands in his pockets.

"What you all need," he said, "is a hatchet."

"Anything else?" asked Kirby, starting for the tool shed.

"A screw driver, and a cup, and—well, I guess that's all."

Big took the hatchet and gave the coconut a whack on the end. Three little cracks appeared. Thrusting the edge of the chisel into a crack, Big began to pry off the thick shell. It came off all brown and hairy, and inside was another brown and hairy nut.

"Aren't we inside *yet?*" cried Bitsy.

"Pretty soon now," said Big.

He held up the inner nut and they saw that the end of it had three small depressions which looked like the eyes and mouth of a monkey. Big took the screw driver and

made holes in two of these. From one of these holes he poured a milky white liquid into the cup.

"Drink that," he said, handing the cup to Kirby. Kirby drank some of the coconut milk, and then he handed the cup to Bitsy.

"Well?" asked Miss Ferry. "How do you like it?"

"It's sort of strange," said Kirby.

"But good," said Bitsy.

"Strange but good," said Miss Ferry, "that's what they used to say about the Pink Motel in Hiram Stonecrop's day."

With a final whack of the hatchet, Big cracked the inner nut, and it fell into exactly four pieces, showing the beautiful white meat inside.

"There you are," said Big, smiling.

"Dear me!" said Miss Ferry. "What a fuss to get inside a coconut. Is it worth it?"

"Yes, it's good," said Kirby. They all began to chip off the fine, white meat and taste its delicious flavor. It really was good.

While they were in the midst of this pleasant occupation, a large, long Super-Duper automobile drove into the motel yard. It was a beautiful two-tone chocolate and coffee-colored car with chrome trimmings. Out of it stepped a very tanned lady and gentleman, dressed in white sports clothes.

On the back seat sat a girl about the age of Kirby and Big, and just a little bit older than Bitsy. She did not move to get out of the car, and she appeared to be very much bored with it all. She was tanned, too, and she had long yellow hair and very blue eyes. She would have been pretty, Bitsy thought, if she had looked interested. To be pretty one really ought to look interested.

"Now you wait right there, Sandra," the lady said to the little girl. "Sit right still and we shall soon be back."

"I was going to," said Sandra.

"And don't try to start the car or get the candy bars out of the glove compartment, darling," said the gentleman.

"I wasn't going to," said Sandra.

"Be good," said both the lady and gentleman together.

Sandra did not bother to answer this time. She just sat still with her nose in the air.

Kirby and Big raced to help the newcomers with their bags and to call Kirby's father.

Bitsy went up beside the car and said, "Hello" to the new girl. But Sandra might have been deaf as far as Bitsy's greeting was concerned. The only sign she gave that she had heard was to raise her nose a quarter of an inch higher in the air.

Miss Ferry had been watching all of this. Now she shook her head, gathered up her canvas and her paints, and went off murmuring, "Too bad! Too bad!" What it was that was too bad, she did not bother to state.

Bitsy tried again. "I said, *hello*. Hi there! Hello!"

"I really didn't notice," Sandra said. "But, if you insist, why then, *hello!*"

Bitsy gave up. She sighed and wandered off to see which cabin the new people would choose. They took the one at

27

the farthest end of the row from the one Miss Ferry had. It was the cabin that had the airplane on top.

"All we wish for is privacy," said the gentleman, whose name was Mr. Brown, "and an opportunity to work at our suntan. We come south every winter to acquire a good coat of tan, and we must not waste a moment of this sunshine. Have you a DO NOT DISTURB sign to hang on our front door?"

"Well, I don't know," said Kirby's father. "The office of the former owner is in quite a mess. The sign may be there, and we just haven't found it. However, we will be very careful not to disturb you. I'll tell the children."

"Thank you very much," said Mr. Brown. "Come now, Sandra. Get right out, dear. We are going to stay."

"Where is the suntan lotion?" asked Mrs. Brown. "Sandra, have you put it somewhere?"

"Right here," said Sandra, handing her mother a bottle. "It's just where you left it."

"Isn't she precious?" said Mrs. Brown to Mr. Brown.

"A truly remarkable girl," replied Mr. Brown, "and remember, she's our very own daughter, dear."

"She's getting a real nice suntan, too," said Mrs. Brown proudly.

Sandra yawned and stepped languidly out of the car. Her long light hair looked almost white against her tanned skin. She tossed it back now, and elevated her small, bored nose an inch higher.

"She isn't very interested in things, is she?" murmured

28

Bitsy. When she had seen a girl in the car, Bitsy had hoped for someone to play with.

There was only one instant, just at the threshold of the airplane cabin, when Sandra gave a quick look around at Bitsy and Kirby and Big that was *almost* interested. But then she went on in, and the children could hear her mother saying, "Now don't go near the water, dear, until Daddy tells you to." And Sandra said, crossly, "I wasn't going to."

"Well!" said Kirby's father, "here are some more odd ones. Cousin Rose Thornapple seems to have been right about the unusual guests." Then he added, "Don't disturb them when they're on the beach, children. And, by the way, Kirby, just look around Uncle Hiram's office, please, and see if you can find a DO NOT DISTURB sign."

"All right, Daddy," Kirby said. He liked nothing better than to be sent into Uncle Hiram's office to hunt for something.

4. An Odd Pencil and Some Valuable Dogs

The office had a pleasing smell of tobacco and fish and camphorated oil, and it seemed to be full of possibilities. The first thing Kirby did when he went into Uncle Hiram's office was to sit down in the swivel chair and twirl himself around. Sometimes he twirled himself around once, sometimes as many as six times. Three good twirls were the usual number.

There was a framed motto over Uncle Hiram's roll-top desk, and for a moment Kirby sat tilted back in the swivel chair and looked up at it. Instead of "Time is money" or "Teach your dollars to have more cents," Uncle Hiram's motto was the poem by Robert Louis Stevenson that everybody learns before he goes to kindergarten:

> The world is so full of a number of things,
> I'm sure we should all be as happy as kings.

There were certainly a number of things cram-jammed into this little office, and when Kirby sat down in Uncle Hiram's swivel chair, twirled himself around three times, and then rolled up the top of the desk, he usually began to feel as happy as a king. This feeling was all a part of the curious magic that seemed to surround the Pink Motel.

Kirby rummaged around among the papers and shells and pipes and steamship folders inside the desk. Almost at once he found a very interesting pencil. It looked like a little cane, because, instead of an eraser, it had a hooked and crooked handle on the end of it.

Now whenever Kirby held a pencil in his hand, he felt compelled to write or draw with it. So, taking firm hold of this one, Kirby started to print his name with it on the back of an envelope. But a very odd thing happened. The pencil seemed to squirm in Kirby's fingers, and, no matter how carefully he tried to print, all of the letters looked like Chinese characters. KIRBY came out

K⦵ᴎ𐐒人

This upset Kirby so much that he put the pencil back, closed the top of the desk and began to look in the drawers. They were stuffed full of everything under the sun. Kirby even found a piece of toast with a bite taken out of it. He decided that *that* could be thrown away anyhow.

Finally in the bottom drawer on the right Kirby found what he was looking for. It was a beautiful sign on a nice stiff piece of cardboard, and it certainly said DISTURB in large letters in the center. Kirby didn't bother to read the smaller printing, but ran with it to Mr. Mellen.

"Here it is, Daddy," he said.

Mr. Mellen took the sign and looked at it carefully. Then he said, "But this says *Please* DISTURB *as often as you like*. I'm afraid it won't do, Kirby."

Kirby took the sign back and put it in the bottom drawer of the desk. It was a beautiful sign and it seemed a pity to put it back. But somehow it was better suited to Uncle Hiram than to the Browns. Reluctantly Kirby closed the desk, gave the swivel chair a twirl and went out of the office.

The sunshine was beautifully warm, and Kirby was pleased with it. He found Big picking up fallen coconuts and adding them to the pile behind the cabin.

"What shall we do with them?" asked Kirby. "I'd hate to have to crack all of them."

"Some people sells 'em," said Big. "But most folks around here got so many, they don't want any more. Especially not if they have to pay for 'em."

32

"If we had them in Minnesota," Kirky said, "we could sell them."

"How far to Minnesota?" asked Big.

"About two thousand miles, I guess."

"That's too far," Big said. "We better think of something else to do with 'em."

"Mama could make a coconut cake," said Bitsy, skipping up hopefully.

"Still we got too many," said Big.

"We'll think of some way to use them," Kirby said. Kirby did not give up easily when he had a problem to solve.

While they were talking, they heard another car drive into the yard.

"More guests already?" Kirby cried.

"Sure enough," said Big. "This the season when they come. Won't any house stand empty long, this time of year."

The three children ran around to the front of the motel to see who was arriving. A small foreign convertible car with the top down had just been driven into the space before the motel and parked beside the Browns' long Super-Duper. When the motor was turned off, there was a shrill sound of barking to be heard. The three children ran up hopefully, and they were delighted to see that the back seat of the car was full of dogs. Actually there were only three dogs, but when they are all barking, three seems like a lot.

The three dogs were miniature poodles. At first Kirby thought that they were all exactly alike. Then he noticed that they had been clipped in different ways so that you could tell them apart. One was clipped to look like a lion, with a bushy mane and a tuft on the tip of his tail. One was clipped smooth down the back, but had long shaggy hair on his legs—like trousers. The third poodle had rings and tufts of hair clipped every which way, and a topknot on her head with a bow of blue ribbon tied to it.

A brisk young lady hopped out of the car and asked Kirby's father about a cabin. The young lady had short dark hair, and she wore large dark glasses over her large dark eyes. She had a very businesslike way of speaking.

"I want a nice place to swim, and I like the looks of your beach very much," she said. "I hope that you do not have any rule against accepting pets. It's perfectly amazing how many stuffy and bad-mannered motels there are along the way that say NO PETS. *No pets*, indeed! I couldn't live without my poochie-pies."

34

"I don't know," said Kirby's father. "We haven't had to decide about pets before this. We really haven't formed a policy regarding them."

"Wait a minute, Daddy," cried Kirby. He remembered a sign he had just seen in the drawer with the DISTURB sign. In a moment he came back with it, and it said, WE WELCOME PETS.

"Ah, yes," said Mr. Mellen. "I see that our policy is to welcome pets. I hope that yours are well-bred."

"Indeed, yes," cried the young lady, whose name was Miss Pamela DeGree. "Every one is a champion. I can show you their papers if you like. The trunk of the car is half full of blue ribbons and silver cups which they have won."

"I really meant, are they well-behaved?" asked Mr. Mellen.

"That, too!" said Miss P. DeGree. "You won't find better-behaved dogs anywhere. Aren't you good dogs, my little angels?"

"Bow!"

"Wow!"

"Yap!" replied the three dogs politely. Kirby thought, however, that they did not look very much interested in good behavior.

"Very well," said Mr. Mellen, "I will put you in cottage number two, the Prancing Horse."

"Good," said Miss DeGree. "I'm quite fond of horses, also, that is, if they are thoroughbreds."

35

"Kirby, please show Miss DeGree to her cabin," Mr. Mellen said.

"Excuse me, but there is one more thing that I shall require," said Miss DeGree. "I shall need a sitter or sitters, also."

"You mean a setter?" asked Mr. Mellen, whose mind was still considerably cluttered up with dogs.

"No, no," said Miss DeGree impatiently. "I mean a sitter or sitters for the times when I wish to go swimming or playing tennis or bowling or to the movies."

Mr. Mellen scratched his head in bewilderment, but Kirby knew exactly what Miss DeGree had in mind.

"You know, Daddy," he cried eagerly, "like a baby sitter, she means, only this would be a sitter for dogs."

"I see," said Mr. Mellen slowly. He had never before heard of anyone requiring a sitter for dogs, but he knew that Kirby was usually right about such things. Still scratching the back of his head, Mr. Mellen thought very hard. Then, looking at Kirby and Bitsy and Big who stood before him in a hopeful row, he had a bright idea. "Yes," he said thoughtfully, "I believe that we can supply you with three sitters, Miss DeGree. One for each dog. What do you say to these three sitters right here?"

Miss DeGree looked the three children over very carefully, then she began to smile. "Splendid!" she said. "I knew by the delightful pink color of this place that I should find exactly what I wanted here."

During this conversation, the dogs had stopped barking. Now, when Kirby looked at them, he saw that they were

36

all yawning. Their pink tongues curled up cunningly on the ends. It occurred to him that they looked as bored as Sandra Brown.

Goodness! Kirby thought, we must do something about this.

"They've been benched at a dog show for two days," said Miss DeGree. "They need exercise. Would the sitters care to walk them?"

The sitters were delighted to do so.

"I am glad that we can be walkers as well as sitters," Bitsy said. The hardest thing for Bitsy to do was to sit still.

"Before you start, of course," said Miss DeGree, "I shall have to introduce you to my angels."

"Naturally," Kirby said. "And I'll tell you who we are. I am Kirby, and this is Bitsy, and this is my friend Big."

"Very good," said Miss DeGree. "Leo, step down and shake hands with Kirby, please." The dog with mane and tail clipped like a lion jumped out of the car obediently, sat on his hind legs and offered his paw to Kirby.

"Now, Pantaloon," said Miss DeGree to the dog with the shaggy legs, "shake hands with Big."

"Pleased to meet you, Panty," said Big, shaking the dog's paw.

"Pant-a-*loon*," corrected Miss DeGree gently.

"Pleased to meet you, Loony," said Big, shaking paws again.

"Oh, dear! dear!" cried Miss DeGree, "the name is *Pantaloon*. I can't have my doggies nicknamed. I don't know what the Kennel Club would think of that."

37

"Pantaloon," repeated Big. "I'll sure try hard to remember, miss."

"And what's mine's name?" asked Bitsy. The poodle, clipped every which way with a blue bow on her topknot, had already shaken paws with Bitsy, and now she was busy tweaking Bitsy's sash untied.

"Her name is Ruffles," Miss DeGree said. "She's the one who usually gets into trouble. Ruffles, behave yourself." Ruffles sat up meekly and yawned.

Miss DeGree snapped a leash on each dog's collar.

"Keep them on their leashes," cautioned Miss DeGree. "They are very, very valuable. I wouldn't want to lose one —not for anything!"

The small dogs stepped daintily, lifting their feet high, as if they still believed that they were competing for blue ribbons. When the children took them walking on the beach, it looked and felt like a parade.

5. Arrival of Two Mysterious Gentlemen

At the other end of the beach, Mr. and Mrs. Brown and Sandra were busily working at their suntan. Mr. and Mrs. Brown lay face downward on large beach towels, so that their backs would get as tanned as their fronts. "Just like real nice pancakes," Mr. Brown said, "evenly done on both sides."

And Mrs. Brown said: "Think how our friends will envy us when we get back up North. We won't even have to tell them we have been on a vacation. They will take one look at us and know."

Sandra did not say anything. She was sitting straight up on her beach towel and looking out to sea with a very bored expression on her face.

"There go those children," said Mr. Brown, raising his head to look down the beach. "I hope that they will not disturb us while we are busy."

Mrs. Brown raised her head and looked also. "Dear me!" she said, "and they have dogs with them. Dogs on the beach! This is really terrible. Don't you think it is terrible, Sandra?"

Without really turning her head (she was much too bored to do a thing like that), Sandra glanced out of the corner of her eye at the other end of the beach. For an instant there came a little glimmer of surprise and interest into her face.

It really did look like a parade down there. Kirby and Leo, Big and Pantaloon, Bitsy and Ruffles were all walking sedately along, one behind the other, under the coco palm trees.

"But it's all right," Mr. Brown said. "They aren't coming this way."

"Good," Mrs. Brown said. "I distinctly heard Mr. Mellen tell them not to disturb us. Apparently they mind well."

Sandra gave a long, long sigh and turned her blue eyes back to the sea. She was just about as brown as any child needed to be, and it seemed to her that she had not done

40

anything interesting in a month of Sundays. Ho-ho-hum.

Quite a long way down the beach, the three children with the dogs came across Miss Elizabeth Ferry painting a picture.

"Kirby, my boy," called Miss Ferry. "Come here a moment, will you? I'm having a dreadful time with this picture. Just draw me one of your funny coco palm trees, won't you, please?"

Kirby came up and drew a palm tree in the sand with a stick.

"Beautiful!" Miss Ferry said. "That is just the thing that I need for the middle of my picture. I think you are a primitive, Kirby."

"A which?" said Kirby.

"Never mind," Miss Ferry said. "I couldn't explain it myself, but it's something nice, I assure you."

The children stood around and watched Miss Ferry while she put Kirby's tree into the middle of her picture with strong black strokes.

"How do you like it?" she asked.

The children were not sure that the picture had been improved, but the dogs certainly seemed pleased. They began to jump around Miss Ferry and bark as if they expected something from her.

"The dogs look as if they knew you," Kirby said.

"Well, certainly," replied Miss Ferry, "the animals all know me. I like them, and they can always tell that. But sometimes it does get a bit tiresome, because they expect me to treat them, and, when I'm painting, I'm likely to forget."

She opened her hamper and found three small pieces of hard-cooked liver which she tossed to the three dogs.

"You, too, I suppose," she said to the children, and took three small raspberry tarts out of the hamper and handed them around. The raspberry tarts were very delicious and simply melted away on the tongue like a blissful dream.

"Animals!" continued Miss Ferry impatiently. "The crabs, for instance, have been bothering me all morning. They are nice little things but very persistent. Would you like to see them dance? They'll do it at the drop of a hat."

"We didn't wear our hats," said Bitsy.

"Never mind," Miss Ferry said. "That's only an old woman's careless way of speaking. Come, crabs," she called.

From holes in the sand, a number of small crabs came scuttling out. They walked sideways on the very tips of their toes, or so it seemed. They waved their feelers and goggled their eyes and ran sideways very fast like ballet dancers. It was comical, to say the least, and the children burst out laughing.

"Hush! hush!" cautioned Miss Ferry. "It isn't funny to them, and you always have to think of the feelings of others."

Politely the children stifled their giggles. They were obliged to hold fast to the ends of the leashes, for all three dogs were straining to get loose and put an end to the crab ballet.

"They won't care if you smile," Miss Ferry said. "Crabs are not that sensitive, but to laugh out loud—well, how would you feel, if you yourself were doing a ballet?"

Presently Miss Ferry said to the crabs, "All right, dears, that's enough. Here's a little something for you, and now run off and don't bother us. Many thanks." From her hamper she produced some flakes of food which she flung among the eager crabs. They scuttled off with it to their pits in the sand. Kirby was curious to know what it was, because he really wondered what crabs ate.

"What do you feed them, Miss Ferry? What do crabs eat?" he asked.

"Crab food, of course," Miss Ferry said. "Can you imagine what else it might be?"

"But I mean—" began Kirby.

"No, no," Miss Ferry said, "you're not mean, dear boy. You're just annoying me a tiny little bit now, because I do want to get on with my work. Take your dogs and skip along now, like good children."

Puzzled, but content, the three children led the three dogs away in the direction of Miss DeGree's cottage.

"Miss Ferry is sort of odd, isn't she?" said Kirby.

"She been comin' here a long time," said Big. "She Mr. Hiram's real good friend."

"I like her," Bitsy said.

"And her raspberry tarts," added Kirby, running his tongue over his teeth in blissful memory. The dogs kept

43

looking back at Miss Ferry as they were led **away**. It was plain to see that they adored her.

Another car was parked in the motel lot when the children returned.

"My goodness!" Kirby said, "folks are certainly coming fast. Do you suppose it's Mr. Carver?"

"Not in a car like that," said Big. "Mr. Carver, he'll come walkin', when he come. He'll have a packsack on his back, and most likely he'll have presents he made himself for ever'body here."

"Mr. Carver sounds like Santa Claus," said Bitsy.

" 'Cept he hasn't got a long white beard," said Big.

"I wish he'd come," said Bitsy, "and carve us a weather vane for the office."

Kirby had been walking around the new car, inspecting it. It was black and shiny and almost as long, low and lovely as the Browns' car. However, theirs was a two-tone job in chocolate and coffee color, while this one was all black.

"Hmm!" Kirby said thoughtfully. "Shatterproof glass and armor plating! Could it be a police car?" He was very much interested. He put his hand in his pocket and found his J. Edgar Hoover Junior G-Man badge, which he hadn't bothered to wear since he came to the Pink Motel. The salt air had begun to tarnish it, and Kirby was reminded that he had better shine it up.

"Don't look like a police car to me," said Big. "No siren horn, no red light on top."

"There's a pair of scissors on the back seat," said Bitsy,

44

peering inside, "and a lot of little scraps of paper. Somebody's been cutting folded paper into lace doilies. Must be children."

"Let's take the dogs to Miss DeGree, and then find out who's come," said Kirby.

Before they reached Miss DeGree's cottage, however, the children saw the new guests coming out of the office with Kirby's father. They were two dark, tall men in dark pin-striped suits. One was very thin and looked as if he might have a troublesome digestion; the other was quite plump and looked as if he might be jolly if he dared.

"Where are the children?" Bitsy asked.

"Children?" repeated the fat man, and the thin man said: "We have no children."

"But someone had been cutting paper lace in the back seat of your car," said Bitsy. "I thought there must be children."

"Jack!" said the thin man crossly to the fat man, "how many times have I told you to pick up your scraps?"

"I'm sorry, Jimmy," the fat man said. "Honest, I am."

"Don't say that word, Jack!" cried the thin man.

"Maybe you're sorry, but never say you're honest. I'm ashamed of you! And how many times have I told you that cutting paper lace looks very odd to other people. In our business, Jack, a person never, never should look odd."

"What *is* your business, please?" asked Mr. Mellen. "You failed to write it on the register. I got the names James Locke and John Black, but I didn't get your business."

"What should we say, Jimmy?" asked the fat man.

"Just put down business," Jimmy Locke said. "We're businessmen."

"Minding our own," added Jack Black with a sheepish smile. "Honest, we are."

"Ssh!" hissed Mr. Locke. "For Pete's sake!"

The three poodles, who had instantly fallen in love with Miss Ferry, seemed to have taken as sudden a dislike to the two new guests. They sniffed at their heels and began to growl and bark.

"Dogs!" said Mr. Locke. "I don't like them. Hold onto their leashes."

"I had a little dog once," said Mr. Black, sighing. "His name was Rover, and he used to do the cutest—"

"Now, Jack, stop it at once!" said Mr. Locke. "You know the minute you begin to get sentimental, you are shot."

"Bang! bang!" said Mr. Black humbly. "Yes, I know, Jimmy. I must never, never let myself get sentimental. *Hon*—no, no, I won't say it."

46

"You can see," said Jimmy Locke to the children, "that neither one of us likes dogs. So keep them away from us."

"These are very, very valuable dogs," said Bitsy. "Miss DeGree said so. They win all kinds of prizes."

Suddenly Mr. Locke began to look interested. "Valuable, you say?"

"That's what she said, Jimmy," said Mr. Black. "Very, very is what she said."

"Hmm!" murmured Mr. Locke thoughtfully.

"Well, perhaps I had better show you to your cabin," Mr. Mellen said. "I have given you number five, the one with the two men sawing wood on the weather vane. It is right next to the Airplane which is occupied by the Brown family. They wish to be very quiet. They are only interested in getting a nice suntan and they do not want to be disturbed."

"Fine!" Mr. Locke said. "We do not want to be disturbed either, do we, Jack?"

"Not if you say we don't, Jimmy," replied Mr. Black. But Kirby thought that the fat man looked rather wistfully at them and the dogs, as if he really might enjoy a bit of society now and then.

"I presume that you have boats for hire?" Mr. Locke said to Kirby's father.

"Oh, yes, indeed," said Mr. Mellen. "Do you intend to go fishing?"

"We certainly do," said Mr. Locke. "We'll probably be out in the boat all day, every day. Would it be possible for your wife to put us up a lunch?"

47

"Of course," Mr. Mellen said. "She's a real good cook, and she will be happy to oblige you, I am sure."

"There's just one more thing," said Mr. Locke. "This is the motel that used to belong to Hiram Stonecrop, isn't it? We want to be sure about that."

"Oh, yes," said Mr. Mellen. "Were you friends of Hiram's? I don't remember seeing your names in his guest book."

"No, we've never been here before," said Mr. Locke.

"But we've heard about old Hiram and his—" began Mr. Black.

"All right, Jack," interrupted Mr. Locke. "Come on now. Mr. Mellen's going to show us to our cabin."

During all of this conversation Kirby had been unusually quiet. But, after the two men disappeared into the Sawyer cabin with Mr. Mellen, Kirby said: "Did you notice the bulges under the coats of their pin-striped suits?"

"Bulges?" repeated Big and Bitsy.

"Yes," said Kirby solemnly. "I think that they are carrying guns."

He took his J. Edgar Hoover Junior G-Man badge out of his pocket and began to polish it on his sleeve.

6. Sandra Begins
To Be Interested

"Well, business is picking up right smartly," Mrs. Mellen said the next morning. "There are only two cabins left unrented, the Dolphin and the Rooster. At the rate people are coming in, we shouldn't have those empty very long."

"I hope Mr. Carver gets here before the cabins are all rented," Bitsy said. "He must make us a weather vane."

"I hope that Marvello comes," said Kirby.

"Marvello? Who is he?"

"Marvello, the Great," said Kirby. "He's the magician. It's in Uncle Hiram's book."

"I don't know about magicians," Mrs. Mellen said. "A magician sounds a little *too* unusual to me. Now those nice, quiet gentlemen who came in yesterday—if only we had more of those!"

"Mama," Kirby said, "I don't like the looks of those

49

men. There's something kind of screwy about those two, I'm sure."

"Screwy?" Mrs. Mellen said. "If you mean that their heads are screwed on in the right direction, you are quite correct. A nice black car, neat dark suits, good manners, not odd in any way—what more can you ask?"

"One of them cuts paper lace," said Bitsy. "Isn't that odd?"

"Well, my goodness!" Mrs. Mellen said, "if they don't do anything worse than that!"

Kirby didn't say anything, for he had to be sure before he made an accusation. But this morning he was wearing his badge, and it was no longer tarnished by the salt air but was polished so that it sparkled in the sunshine.

"Now, don't forget, children," said Mrs. Mellen, "that you're to sit with the dogs again this morning. Miss De-Gree is going into town to get her hair done."

"Mama, we won't forget," the children said.

The three dogs wagged their tails politely in greeting when they saw the three children, but at the same time they yawned and stretched as if they found life dull.

"Be sure to keep them on their leashes," cautioned Miss DeGree. "They are—"

"—very, very valuable," chorused the children.

Of course Kirby took charge of Leo; Big took Pantaloon, and Bitsy took Ruffles, just as on the day before. Miss DeGree had given all of the dogs baths, and Kirby thought that they were the cleanest little dogs that he had ever seen, and also the best behaved. They minced along

50

at the ends of their leashes, staring straight ahead and lifting their feet daintily.

"Our old dog Spot, he wouldn't know what to make of these here," said Big laughing. When Big laughed, he looked so pleasant that Kirby and Bitsy had to laugh, too.

"I didn't know you had a dog," Kirby said.

"Yes, sir!" Big said. "Spot's a hound dog with floppy ears. He's a hunting dog. If you want a coon or a rabbit or a alligator, Spot sure get it for you."

"You mean a real, live alligator?" Kirby asked.

"Sure enough," said Big. "We got a plenty of 'em in the swamp back behind our house."

"Golly!" said Kirby, and Bitsy said, "Then Spot must be a very, very valuable dog, too."

"Well, he sure don't look like these little dogs," laughed Big. "Sometime you all come to my house, and you can see him for yourselves."

"We will," Kirby said. "I sure would like to see a live alligator."

"Spot, too," said Bitsy.

"But you know what I think?" said Kirby. "I think we should do something to give these poodles a good time. They don't look to me as if they had ever had any fun. They don't know how to play."

"We might ask Miss Ferry how to amuse them," suggested Bitsy. "She would know."

"If we had her lunch basket," said Big, "we could give them snacks."

"Us, too!" said Kirby. "Mmmm! Raspberry tarts!"

51

"Raspberry tarts! Mmmm!" cried all three children together.

"Where do you reckon she gets her snacks?" asked Big. "I never see her do no cookin'."

"And she left her wand in the broom closet in her New York apartment," said Bitsy.

"She was only joking about that," said Kirby.

"I know what we'll do to amuse the dogs," said Bitsy. "I'll get my doll trunk, and we'll dress them up in doll clothes."

"That won't be fun for them!" said Kirby. "Or us either!"

"Of course it will," said Bitsy. "Let's try it. We've got to begin somewhere to teach them how to play. Here, hold Ruffles' leash a minute while I get my doll clothes."

"Girls have the silliest ideas," said Kirby to Big.

"Sure do," said Big. "I got five sisters, so I know."

In a moment Bitsy was back with a small trunk of doll clothes. *"Now!"* she said, bustling around. Before they knew it, the two boys found themselves sitting beneath a coco palm tree helping Bitsy dress poodle dogs in doll clothes. They were quite surprised at themselves. The dogs were surprised also. Nothing like that had ever been done to them before. They had been washed and combed and paraded up and down before judges at dog shows, but they had never been dressed in doll clothes.

Bitsy was in her element, telling everybody how to play and what to do next.

52

"Now this is my house," Bitsy said, "and Ruffles is my child. Each of you must have a house, too, and then you must bring your children over to call on us and we will have a tea party."

"That's girls' play," objected Kirby. But Big only laughed.

"Girls have fun, too," Big said.

"If you play girls' play with me," bargained Bitsy, "sometime I will play boys' play with you."

"Well," said Kirby, "it's silly, and I don't know who thinks it's a way to have a good time. But okay."

At the other end of the beach Mr. and Mrs. Brown and Sandra were lying on the sand working at their suntan. Bitsy was in a managing mood this morning, and when she looked in that direction, she could not bear to see Sandra doing nothing but toasting herself.

"That Sandra," Bitsy said, "I think she ought to play with us, too. She's just wasting her time lying there. I think I'll go get her."

"You know what Daddy said about disturbing them," warned Kirby. "And anyway she'll just put her nose up higher in the air."

"Don't guess that nose of hers can go no higher," said Big.

"I'll be real polite," Bitsy said. "Come on, Ruffles."

Ruffles found it difficult to walk sedately with a red calico doll's skirt flapping around her hind legs. To keep from tripping, she began to prance and bounce at the end of her leash. Next she began to bark. She had a yellow sunbonnet tied around her ears, and she looked quite comical, prancing and bouncing.

Sandra was not even gazing out to sea today. She lay in a dump of boredom with her long blond hair falling over her face. She was even too bored to say "Ho-hum."

"Now, Sandra darling," Mrs. Brown said, "turn just a little so you will tan evenly."

And Mr. Brown said, "Not too much, dear, or you might miss a spot."

Bitsy stopped in front of the Browns and said politely to Mrs. Brown, "Excuse me, but can Sandra come out?"

Mrs. Brown looked up from her sunning in surprise.

"Why, she *is* out," Mrs. Brown said, and she added to Mr. Brown, "Here's one of those children, dear, and a dog, too."

"I mean, can she come and play?" explained Bitsy. "Once in a while she really ought to play."

"Well, she may if she wishes to," Mrs. Brown said, "but I'm sure she wouldn't want to, would you, Sandra dear?"

Sandra had pushed back her hair and was peeping through it. Ruffles in a red petticoat and yellow bonnet was almost enough to make her laugh. Not quite. Yet she was starting to be interested. Slowly Sandra sat up and tossed her hair behind her ears.

"I might," she said.

"Darling," said Mrs. Brown to Mr. Brown, "Sandra says that she might."

"Might what?" asked Mr. Brown, sitting up in alarm.
"Whatever it is, she had better be careful."

"She says she might play with these children and dogs."

"Good heavens!" said Mr. Brown. "She can't mean it,
can she?"

"Sandra dear, do you really mean it?" Mrs. Brown
asked.

"I'm thinking about it," Sandra said.

"Oh, come along, do!" said Bitsy impatiently. "We're
having a keen time. We're dog sitting this morning."

"What do you think, dear?" Mrs. Brown asked Mr.
Brown.

"The dogs look well bred," said Mr. Brown, "but I
don't know about the children."

"Please come along," urged Bitsy. "It's just down the
beach in plain sight."

"All right," Sandra said. "I will."

"Do you hear that, dear? Sandra says that she will!" cried Mrs. Brown.

"Fantastic!" exclaimed Mr. Brown.

"Ho-hum," said Sandra, stifling a yawn. She got up and dusted the sand off her bathing suit. "Let's go," she said.

"If you get the least bit cold, come back for your sweater, Sandra," called Mrs. Brown after her.

"And your rubbers if it starts to rain," called Mr. Brown.

It had not been hard at all to get Sandra to come.

"They seem to worry about you quite a lot," said Bitsy, as she and Sandra walked down the beach.

"Yes, it gets rather burdensome at times," Sandra said. "They mean well, but they haven't anything but me to worry about."

"You mean they don't have to worry about making money or keeping the wolf from the door or anything like that?" asked Bitsy.

"Well, of course, they have their suntan to worry about," Sandra said, "but I am a much more important worry than that."

"I should think so," Bitsy said admiringly. "You look very important, Sandra."

"I am," Sandra said calmly.

"It must make you happy to be very important," Bitsy said. "Kirby and I have fun, but we are not very important."

56

"Oh, I don't know about being happy," Sandra said. "But aren't you and Kirby important at all?"

Bitsy tried to think how she and Kirby could possibly be important; then she remembered Uncle Hiram's secret.

"We are important because our motel has a secret."

"Really?" asked Sandra, looking just a little bit interested. "What kind of secret?"

"We don't know," said Bitsy.

"You mean you won't tell. Is that it?" Sandra asked.

"No, we really don't know," said Bitsy.

"Well!" said Sandra haughtily, "I don't see how you can feel important over a secret you don't know."

"But if you *know* a secret," Bitsy said, "it isn't a secret any more, is it?"

"Maybe not," Sandra admitted.

It turned out to be a very pleasant morning for everyone. The dogs forgot to yawn, Sandra forgot to be bored, and Kirby, Bitsy and Big always had a good time anyway. After they had tried all the clothes that would fit on all of the dogs, they thought of other things which pleased the boys more. They ran races on the beach, and then they dug holes in the damp sand near the water and watched the sea fill them up. The dogs were particularly good at digging holes. Their small, clean feet got wet and sandy. They enjoyed this even more than wearing doll clothes, it seemed.

The children found shells, and Sandra even thought that she might begin to make a collection. Sometimes for several moments she forgot about keeping her nose in the air.

Once when Kirby looked out to sea, he noticed that a small boat was anchored a short distance from shore. Two men in the boat were leaning over the side and looking into the water as if they had lost something.

"It's those men who came in yesterday," said Kirby, "Mr. Black and Mr. Locke."

"I wonder if they catch a lot of fish," said Big.

"It doesn't look as if they were fishing at all," Kirby said. "I don't see any fishing rods."

"Oh, yes, they got 'em," Big said, "but it don't look like they using them."

"They're looking for something under the water," Sandra said. "What a tiresome business that would be. There's such a lot of water!"

"But water has interesting things in it," Bitsy said, "shells and jellyfish, and sand dollars—"

"Sand dollars?" Kirby said. "Maybe they're looking

for *real* dollars. Didn't Miss Ferry say the pirates and the Spaniards used to hide their treasure around here?"

"Well, she said some people thought so," said Bitsy. "*She* didn't think that was Uncle Hiram's secret. *She* thought his secret was something he had learned."

"But what if these men knew something that we didn't know?" Kirby asked.

"I don't believe your uncle had a secret," Sandra Brown said.

"Oh, yes, he did," said Big. "Everyone who knew Mr. Stonecrop felt right sure of that."

As the children watched, the two men in the boat pulled up the anchor and began to row around the point of land beyond the beach.

"I don't think they found anything," Bitsy said.

"Well, really," said Sandra, "what can you expect? It's just two very ordinary men out fishing."

"They are not as ordinary as they want us to think," said Kirby. "I feel as if I've seen those men somewhere before, and I don't like the looks of them."

"That's what you told Mama," Bitsy said.

"And it's what I still think, too," said Kirby.

7. The Great Marvello

Another gentleman arrived at the Pink Motel that afternoon, and Mr. Mellen put him in the Dolphin cabin. Nobody saw this third gentleman arrive. Suddenly he was there—with a very large trunk covered with foreign labels, and six hatboxes of different sizes. It was presumed that he had arrived in a taxicab; yet nobody had heard a taxi either driving up or departing. This was not strange, however, as the wind was blowing and the waves were making a loud roar. Also the palm leaves were flapping and the weather vanes were going whiz, whirr, snap and bang.

Something about the mysterious arrival of this tall gentleman with a pointed beard interested the children very much. They had returned the dogs to Miss DeGree by that time, and they were free to stand around with slightly opened mouths and watch Mr. Mellen welcome the new guest.

Although it was a very warm day, the stranger wore a long dark blue cape lined with scarlet. He had wonderful eyebrows which went up and down when he asked a question. Kirby also saw with pleasure that the stranger was able to wiggle his ears. This was an accomplishment which Kirby himself had only just mastered.

Up and down went the stranger's eyebrows as he asked his first question:

"Where, may I inquire, is my friend Hiram Stonecrop?"

"I am sorry to say," said Kirby's father, "that poor old Hiram has passed away."

"Alas!" cried the stranger, "this is sad news indeed. And Miss Ferry? She has not passed away also, I hope?"

The children all cried out at this. "Oh, no! Miss Ferry is here. She's very much alive."

"Yes," said Kirby's father. "Miss Ferry is in cabin number one, the Duck. That is, unless she is out painting."

"Good!" the gentleman said. "If both Hiram and Elizabeth Ferry had gone, I should not have remained either. The place would not have seemed the same."

Kirby began to feel excited. "Oh, sir," he cried, "are you—? Can you be—?"

Just then Miss Ferry came along, carrying a freshly painted canvas in her hand. When she saw the new arrival, she dropped the canvas and held out both of her hands.

"Marvello!" she cried. "The Great Marvello! How perfectly delightful to see you. It's been a long time, hasn't it?"

61

"Alas, yes!" the Great Marvello said. "I've been touring all the capitals of Europe, and that takes time. I'm really exhausted. I can scarcely find a rabbit in a hat any more, I'm that tired. And whenever I need a rest, this is the place I come to. You know that."

"Yes, I know," Miss Ferry said. "But I expect you've heard the melancholy news of Hiram's passing."

"Yes, I just heard. I shouldn't have stayed at all, after hearing that, except that you are here. And the place is the same color, the same fabulous pink."

"We intend to change the color as soon as possible," said Kirby's father hastily. But neither Marvello nor Miss Ferry heard him. They were so pleased to see each other that they went right on talking.

"Such a delightful color!" Marvello said. "Things can't have changed too much since Hiram's day if the Motel is still pink."

"No, no," Miss Ferry said. "These people seem to be very nice They are distantly related to Hiram. (Don't you think the little boy resembles him a trifle?) I don't believe they mean to change things very much."

"Did Hiram leave them his secret?"

"Unfortunately not," Miss Ferry said. "I am so afraid that the secret may be lost forever."

"Nothing is ever really lost," the Great Marvello said. "It is only temporarily misplaced, out of sight, sleight of hand, you know."

Kirby had been listening to this conversation with great interest.

62

"Are you the magician, sir?" he asked. He had been trying to ask it for some time.

"Yes, I am—that is, I *was*. The magic is not running very strongly in me these days."

"It will come back," Miss Ferry said.

"Could you—could you show us a trick?" asked Kirby breathlessly. Since Kirby was an amateur magician himself, it was thrilling for him to meet a real one.

"Well, I suppose so," said the Great Marvello. He took out a deck of cards and asked Kirby to select one without showing him what it was. Kirby selected the queen of spades and slipped it back into the deck. Marvello shuffled the deck and then cut and held up a card. "Is this your card?" he asked. It was the queen of hearts instead of the queen of spades. Forgetting his manners, Kirby was just starting to say, "I could do better than that myself," but Miss Ferry held up a warning finger.

"Kirby dear," she said, "would you please pick up my painting? I accidentally dropped it in my excitement at seeing an old friend."

Kirby picked up Miss Ferry's painting and held it out to her. The fresh paint was all coated and stuck with sand.

"Oh, look!" he said. "It's covered with sand."

"My dear Miss Ferry," cried Marvello, "you have spoiled your picture, and all because of me. Let me see if I can wipe off some of the sand." He began to take a thin silk handkerchief out of his pocket. It was a bright red one, and attached to it was a blue one, followed by a

63

yellow, a purple, a green and an orange one. The final handkerchief of the string was colored like a flag.

Just as Marvello was starting to wipe the sand away, Miss Ferry cried, "Stop!" They all stopped and looked. Big and Bitsy and Kirby and Mr. and Mrs. Mellen. They all stood around and looked at Miss Ferry's picture.

There was the bright-colored paint she had first put on it, and there were curious ridges and creases of sand, and now stuck brightly here and there were the many-colored silk handkerchiefs with the flag stuck gaily in the center.

"It's perfect!" Miss Ferry cried happily. "Please don't touch it, anyone. I shall call it 'Tribute to the Flag,' and I am sure that they will hang it in the next art show. That is, if you will allow me to keep your handkerchiefs, Marvello."

"Keep them," Marvello said. "I have a great many more; and I'm only too happy to have benefited your picture. The way I feel now, I shall probably never use any of my silk handkerchiefs again anyway. I am at a very low ebb."

"You'll be surprised what a few days at the Pink Motel will do for you," Miss Ferry said. "You must not allow yourself to become discouraged."

"I'll teach you all the tricks that I know," Kirby said generously. After the failure of the card trick, Kirby felt that the magician really did need help.

"Thank you," Marvello said. "That is very kind of you. And now I think that I shall retire into my cabin for a short siesta. Kirby, will you kindly carry in my trunk?"

"I'll try," said Kirby, casting a dubious eye on the trunk.

"I'll help," said Big.

Kirby and Big took hold of the magician's very large trunk, expecting it to be very heavy. But it was as light as a feather, and it practically floated into the cabin by itself. Because of its size, there was some little difficulty in getting it through the door, but, by pushing and prodding it here and they, they found that they could make it go through.

Once inside the cabin, the two boys were surprised to see that there was a white rabbit sitting on the table and two white doves were roosting on the top of the electric lamp.

"What will mama say to that?" Kirby wondered. But then he remembered Uncle Hiram's sign WE WELCOME PETS, and so he did not make any fuss about the rabbit and the doves.

"Thank you, boys, thank you!" Marvello said, as they put his trunk into one corner of the room. "Pardon me," he added, "but each of you has something sticking out of his ear."

The boys put their hands up to their ears, but they could feel nothing at all. They were much surprised when Marvello took a shiny new quarter out of each boy's ear.

"Easy come, easy go," Marvello said, as he handed each boy the quarter that he had plucked from his ear. Kirby and Big thanked the magician, and Kirby said, "I think your magic is working pretty well again, Mr. Marvello."

"That wasn't bad, was it?" Marvello said. "The trouble is, the magic is not always there when I want it. Now you see it, and now you don't see it. I really must rest and take the sea air. I hope thus to recapture the full use of my powers."

Kirby was really thrilled to have a magician living in the Pink Motel.

"Even if he did fail on the card trick," Kirby said to Bitsy, "it's pretty wonderful to have a magician around. And he's got a white rabbit and white doves, too. I saw them myself."

"And think what he did to Miss Ferry's picture," Bitsy said.

66

"It sure looked mighty messy," said Big.

"But Miss Ferry was pleased," said Bitsy. "She works so hard at her painting, but it doesn't always seem to come out right to suit her."

"Everything else seems easy for her," said Kirby.

"If only she hadn't left her wand at home in her broom closet!" mused Bitsy.

"Now, Bitsy," Kirby said, "you know she told us that was just a joke."

"I know," said Bitsy. "But it would be so much fun if she *did* have a wand, wouldn't it?"

8. Something Is Missing

Kirby kept thinking about the two quiet men in dark pin-striped suits with bulges under their coats. Somehow they looked very familiar to him, although he could not tell why. He consulted the book of Hiram Stonecrop's Friends, and he saw that Jack Black and Jimmy Locke had never visited the Pink Motel before. They had written Chicago as their place of residence. Still that did not help Kirby's memory, because he did not know anyone from Chicago, nor anyone by the name of Black or Locke.

These two men rarely spoke to anyone at the Motel. Early every morning they changed their dark suits for sports outfits with plaid woolen jackets, and went out in a boat to fish. Kirby noticed two things about Mr. Black and Mr. Locke which seemed to him to be clues. The first thing Kirby noticed was that although they spent the whole day out in a boat they never brought in any fish.

"I guess you didn't have much luck today, did you?" Kirby asked, one evening, when they came in.

"No, no luck," said Mr. Black.

"How did you know we didn't?" asked Mr. Locke suspiciously.

"Why, no fish," said Kirby.

"Fish?" inquired Mr. Black in surprise.

"Fish, Jack," said Mr. Locke, "you know, those things that swim around under water. No, no fish."

"Oh, fish," said Mr. Black. "No, no fish."

Without saying anything more, they went into their cabin. But Kirby now got his second important clue. Under the plaid jackets, the two men had the same strange bulges which he had noticed under their pin-striped coats.

"They are carrying guns!" Kirby said to himself. "They wear holsters under their jackets, and they never go any place without them."

Kirby knew all about guns. Hadn't he been the quickest on the draw of any boy in his neighborhood at the age of five years? Although he was now more interested in rockets and space ships, he had never forgotten what he knew about guns. Most of what he knew he had learned from watching television.

When he was very, very small, Kirby had sometimes had to ask his mother which were the bad men and which were the good men in the TV pictures, because they all carried guns and they all looked pretty much alike. But, as Mrs. Mellen herself was rarely able to tell him which were which, Kirby had been obliged to learn for himself by careful watching. He thought that the good men were usually clean and wore neckties, while the bad men needed shaving and did not wear ties. The gangsters, however, were different. They were clean shaven and wore neckties like the good men. But there was one way you could tell them from the good men. They had bulges under their coats!

Now Kirby thought to himself, "Television! That's where I've seen these men, or some just like them!" When he was sure that he knew what they were, he ran in to tell his parents.

"Mother, Daddy," Kirby cried breathlessly, as soon as he was inside the central cabin, "you know those men in the wood sawer cabin? They're gangsters."

"Tut-tut, Kirby!" said Mr. Mellen. "You must be careful what you call people."

"Gangsters, dear!" said Mrs. Mellen. "Don't be foolish. You know yourself that one of them cuts paper lace. He's using up all the pink notepaper in the desk drawer that way. It's a dreadful waste of notepaper. I find all the scraps in the wastebasket."

"Cutting up notepaper?" Mr. Mellen asked. "Dear me, we can't afford that."

"Still it *is* pretty," Mrs. Mellen said. "Look. I saved this out of the wastebasket." She held up a piece of pink notepaper which had been folded many times and cut into a most delightful pattern of leaves and flowers. When it was unfolded, it looked like a pink lace doily instead of a piece of motel writing paper.

70

"But Mama—" Kirby said.

"When I was a girl," continued Mrs. Mellen, "there used to be an old gentleman with long white hair who would come once a year and sit in the window of the drugstore on the corner. His long white hair was really very beautiful, and he sat in the store window to advertise a certain kind of hair tonic."

"But what, my dear," asked Mr. Mellen, "does hair tonic have to do with the waste of the motel notepaper?"

"Oh, didn't I tell you?" Mrs. Mellen asked. "Why, the dear old gentleman used to cut paper lace as he sat in the window. All of us children would line up outside to watch him, and sometimes he would beckon one of us in, and give us one of the lovely doilies he had cut."

"Did he sell much hair tonic?" asked Mr. Mellen.

"As to that, I cannot say," replied Mrs. Mellen. "I'm sure that *I* never bought any."

"Mother! Daddy!" Kirby cried. "I'm telling you that we have gangsters!"

"Impossible," said Mr. Mellen. "This is a very well-run motel."

71

"Besides, Kirby dear," objected Mrs. Mellen, "how would you recognize a gangster?"

"My goodness, Mama," Kirby said, "don't you think I can tell a gangster when I see one? I've watched them often enough on TV."

"One good thing about Florida," Kirby's father said, "is that the boy can play outside in the winter. He doesn't have to spend so many hours indoors watching TV."

Kirby's mother suddenly began to be excited. "So here in Florida we have gangsters in our *motel*," she cried, "instead of on our TV! Is that an improvement?"

"Possibly not," said Mr. Mellen. "Kirby, are you sure?"

"Yes, I'm sure," said Kirby, "and I think they're looking for something, too. All of us children have noticed. They go out all day long in the boat and row around looking and looking. They never bring in any fish."

"Merciful heavens!" said Kirby's mother. "We can't have gangsters! We must ask them to leave at once."

"How can we do that?" asked Mr. Mellen sensibly. "I suppose you want me to go to their cabin and say, 'My dear sirs, you seem to be nice, quiet gentlemen and you have paid your rent in advance, but my son thinks you are gangsters. Therefore, you must leave at once.' It would be most embarrassing."

"Well, of course, we don't want to be embarrassed," Mrs. Mellen said doubtfully. "Besides, we still have one vacant cabin, and, if these gentlemen left, there would be two vacant cabins."

"And if they really are gangsters," Mr. Mellen said, "we don't want to make them angry with us. If those bulges really are guns——"

"Oh, dear!" said Mrs. Mellen. "This is a frightful situation. I am sure, Kirby, that you must be mistaken."

"Well, I hope so," Kirby said, "because gangsters can be quite dangerous."

"We will wait a few days," Mr. Mellen said, "before we do anything. In the meantime, Kirby, just keep your eye on these fellows."

"All right, Daddy, I will," said Kirby.

"And Kirby——"

"Yes, Daddy?"

"Just look in Uncle Hiram's desk and see if you can discover whether he had any general policy with regard to gangsters, will you? You seem to be better than anyone else at turning up information from Uncle Hiram's desk."

Kirby went into the cubbyhole office and sat down in Uncle Hiram's swivel chair. He rolled up the top of the desk. What a delightful mess! It never failed to please and interest Kirby. But, look as he might, he didn't find

a word about gangsters. The nearest thing to the subject that he could find was a sheet of pink paper on which was written in large firm letters, *Honesty is the best policy.*

One thing disturbed him, however. It is true that Uncle Hiram's desk was a terribly untidy mess, but Kirby had looked at it often enough to know just how the mess was arranged. Now he realized that things had been completely turned over and rearranged. Somebody had recently been looking through the contents of Uncle Hiram's desk, and that somebody had not been Kirby. Who could it have been? Black and Locke? The Great Marvello? Miss Ferry? At first, Kirby thought that nothing was missing, but then he remembered the pencil with the crooked handle, like a cane, that had made him write his name so oddly. Today it was not there at all. Kirby closed the desk uneasily. He felt considerably disturbed. Something strange was certainly going on here.

9. Alligator Hunt

First thing the next morning Bitsy ran to find Kirby. "In half an hour Miss DeGree is going to leave the dogs with us while she goes away to play golf. How shall we amuse the dogs today?"

"I don't know," said Kirby absently. His mind was still occupied with thoughts of gangsters and the mystery of Uncle Hiram's desk. Mr. and Mrs. Mellen did not seem to be a great help in the matter, and Kirby knew that he would have to think it out for himself. There is never any better way of solving a problem than to think it out for yourself. Hadn't he read that on a slip of pink paper in Uncle Hiram's desk?

If they were looking for the secret, he thought, the first thing they would do is to rummage through the desk. Perhaps they found a map. I wonder? I never found one, that's sure. But there's no telling what may be missing besides the pencil.

"You don't look very interested, Kirby," Bitsy said. "What I thought was, the dogs must get tired of never meeting any other dogs. Why don't we take them over to see Big's dog Spot? I've been wanting to go and see Big's brothers and sisters anyway. Wouldn't that be fun, Kirby?"

"It would be fun," Kirby said, "but remember these are very, very valuable dogs. Would Miss DeGree like us to take them away from the motel?"

"I asked her," Bitsy said, "and she told me it would be all right, if we kept them on their leashes."

"Where *is* Big today?" asked Kirby. "I haven't seen him."

"Well, we'll find out why he hasn't come," Bitsy said.

"But without Big, who is going to take care of Pantaloon?"

"My goodness, Kirby. You can think of more things. We'll just have to get Sandra, that's all. She's already lying on the beach looking bored to death. I'll run and ask her."

Sandra sat up when she saw Bitsy coming.

"Are you going to play dress-the-dogs-in-doll-clothes again?" asked Sandra, "because I have a little straw hat that would be cute on Pantaloon if we cut holes for his ears to come through." Sandra looked quite interested. Even Mr. and Mrs. Brown looked slightly interested.

"Fine!" said Bitsy, "you can put the hat on him so the

76

sun won't get in his eyes, but we're going to do something different today."

"Different?" asked Sandra.

"Yes, we like to do different things every day," Bitsy said. "It makes life more interesting."

"Something different every day," said Mrs. Brown. "Did you hear that, darling?"

"Yes, I did," said Mr. Brown. "It's a novel idea, isn't it? But do you think that Sandra can stand all these different kinds of things?"

"She looked quite well and happy when she came in yesterday."

"Sandra," asked Mr. Brown, "do you want to do something different again today, so soon?"

"I think so," Sandra said. "It depends on what it is. What is it, Bitsy?"

"Well, today we're going to take the dogs to call on Big's dog Spot. Big lives on the canal, down the road a piece."

"Should we let her go?" asked Mrs. Brown.

"If she is very careful," Mr. Brown said. "If they are all very, very careful, I don't see why not."

"But keep clean, dear," said Mrs. Brown, and, "Don't be late for lunch," said Mr. Brown. "Be good!" cried both of them together.

Big and his family lived down the road a quarter of a mile from the Pink Motel. Their house was about the size of one of the motel cabins, but it was up on stilts. This was because the house was built on the side of a canal and sometimes the water came high onto the bank. If their house had not been on stilts, the high water might have entered the front door and wet their furniture.

A big live oak tree, with festoons of Spanish moss and three rope swings in it, shaded the house. Although it was small, Kirby thought that it was the kind of house he would enjoy living in.

Apparently Big's family enjoyed living in it, because there was a sound of laughter from inside the house, and somewhere out behind there was a sound of singing.

"Big!" called Kirby. "Come out, Big. We came to see you!"

Immediately smiling faces appeared in all the windows. Then five very small children ran out and stood in a row on the front porch. They were like stair steps, each one a little bit smaller than the one before, and all of them were smaller than Big. It was easy now to see how Big got his name. The three poodle dogs began to bark when they saw the children.

Now Big's mother appeared in the doorway. "Good morning," she said.

"Good morning," answered Kirby politely. "Is Big here, please? We came to see him."

"Big and Spot, they've gone alligator hunting," Big's mother said. "They just a little piece up the canal. You go along the path, you find 'em very quick."

"Alligator hunting?" asked Sandra. "Is *that* the different thing we're going to do today?" It was the first time that Kirby and Bitsy had ever seen her really interested and excited.

"Yes, Big went out right early this morning," Big's mother said. "Little alligator been botherin' our ducks. But Spot'll catch him all right. When they catch him, then Big can go to work up at the Pink Motel."

Just then they heard a dog barking away up the canal. The dog's voice was deep and musical. The three miniature poodles began to bark again in their high, shrill voices and to strain on their leashes. Kirby had never seen them so excited.

"Is it safe?" he asked Big's mother. "I mean for girls and dogs?"

"Oh, yes, it safe," said Big's mother, "if you know how to take care of yourselves. But girls and dogs can stay here if they wish to do so."

But Sandra and Pantaloon were already running along the path in the direction of Spot's barking, and Bitsy and Ruffles were right behind them.

"Bitsy, you better come back here," Kirby called. "This is for boys."

"I told you I'd play boy's play with you, if you'd play doll clothes with me," Bitsy called back. "Remember?"

The only thing Kirby could do was to hope for the best, and follow along as fast as he and Leo could go.

The trees arched over the path beside the water. Spanish moss hung down in long ghostly garlands. The path grew more and more slippery and muddy. Soon Spot's barking sounded close by, and around the next bend in the path the children saw Big and Spot splashing around in the muddy water at the edge of the swamp.

The three children and the three poodles ran up shouting and barking. They stood along the slippery bank in a noisy row.

"Bow!"

"Wow!"

"Yap!" shrilled the poodles.

"Hey, Big!"

"We came—"

"To see you!" shouted the children.

Big did not seem as pleased to see them as they had expected he would be.

"I just about had him," Big said. "Now you all scared him away."

"You mean the alligator?" shouted Kirby. "Did you nearly get him?"

"What does an alligator look like?" asked Bitsy fearfully.

"I know," Sandra said. "My mother's got an alligator handbag with a head on it. It has glass eyes and it's smiling."

"Sure," Big said, "alligator smiles all right, but it's a mighty mean smile. When a alligator smiles, that's when you better start to watchin' out for yourself."

"Look!" Kirby cried. "There he goes." He had seen something moving just under the surface of the shallow water. Kirby was so excited that he splashed right into the water with Big and Spot. Leo went in with him. Sandra and Pantaloon were right behind them.

Bitsy did not really want to get into the muddy water, but before she knew what was happening, Ruffles had pulled her in.

Everybody made a rush for the alligator. There was a wonderful splashing and barking and shouting. The muddy water flew in every direction.

As soon as she could, Bitsy climbed out and stood on the bank screaming. She had lost her hold of Ruffles' leash, and, in fact, all of the very, very valuable poodles seemed to be loose, and were splashing around in the mud puddle, barking like crazy.

"Oh, it's smiling! It's smiling!" wailed Bitsy in despair. She had caught a glimpse of the alligator as it came to the surface for an instant amongst all the splashing and shouting.

Big and Kirby both saw the alligator at the same time. Both made a dive for it, and both felt sure they had captured it. Certainly each one of them had caught hold of

81

something. They bobbed up triumphantly, only to discover that they were holding onto each other instead of the alligator.

"Shucks!" said Big, and Kirby said, "Pete's sake!" They stood there glaring at each other. "Done lost him again!" said Big.

Now so much muddy water was being splashed around that nobody could see what was happening. The dogs wallowed and barked, the children scrambled and yelled. But in a minute Sandra gave a triumphant shout. There she stood, knee deep in water, with the four dogs jumping and howling around her. She was covered with mud from head to toe.

"I got it!" Sandra shouted. "I did. I got it all my-

self." She held up a small gray alligator by its tail. "What had I better do with it?"

"Drop it!" advised Bitsy, who found that she much preferred playing dolls to this sort of thing. But Big and Kirby cried, "Hold onto it! Don't let it go!"

Big clamped his hands around the alligator's jaw so that it could not bite them, and Kirby caught hold of its middle.

"Sandra, you sure a good alligator hunter," said Big admiringly.

Everyone could see that Sandra was smiling a wide, delighted smile. It was the only part of her face that was not covered with mud.

"Well!" said Sandra proudly, "it wasn't hard. I just caught it by the tail, and there it was. I did it all myself. It really wasn't hard."

Even Bitsy came close to the edge of the water to see what they had caught. The alligator rolled an eye at them, and he did seem to be smiling, but not pleasantly. Bitsy was very tenderhearted with animals, and already she began to feel sorry for the alligator.

"Don't hurt him!" cried Bitsy. "Poor little thing!"

"We won't hurt him," Kirby said. "Big, can we take him up to the Pink Motel?"

"Sure, you can take him," Big said. "We glad to get rid of him."

"How will we keep him?" asked Bitsy nervously. "I don't want to find him crawling around in my bed at night."

"What do *you* think, Sandra?" asked Kirby. "He's really yours."

"If we could find a nice big box for him," said Sandra, "so he would have room to move around without getting away."

"Marvello's trunk would be the very thing," said Kirby, "but I don't suppose he'd let us take it."

"That trunk of Marvello's," said Big, "I wouldn't trust that trunk to hold anything I want to keep. It float around too light. But I know what. Mr. Hiram, he had a great big ol' box like a trunk out back somewhere. Nobody use it for a long time. It make a real good alligator house."

They found the box, as Big promised, in the swampy place at the far side of the motel. It was among the gumbo limbo trees and palmettos in a place where no one would think of looking.

"My goodness!" Kirby said. "It looks like a pirate's chest." The box was made of oak studded with brass nails and bound with heavy leather straps. It did look like a treasure chest of some sort. The children were impressed.

"Ain't nothin' in it though," said Big.

The box was, in fact, quite empty, and it had several small holes in it, so there was no danger that the alligator would smother when the lid was closed.

"What are we going to feed him?" asked Bitsy anxiously.

"Miss Ferry will know," said Kirby. "Or we may find something in Uncle Hiram's desk about the care and feeding of baby alligators."

84

"Is this a baby?" asked Bitsy.

"He's not very large," said Kirby.

"He seems large when you have him by the tail," said Sandra.

"He plenty large enough," said Big.

"For what?" asked Bitsy.

"Any kind of thing," replied Big.

"He'll have to have water as well as food," said Sandra.

"We can put a pan of water in the chest," Kirby said, "and we should take him out every day for a swim."

"Won't he get away?"

"Maybe he could put him on a leash," said Bitsy.

"*Leashes!*" cried Kirby, striking a muddy hand to his muddy forehead.

In the alligator excitement everybody had forgotten about the very, very valuable poodles and their leashes.

The children looked around now in consternation. But there were the three poodles, safe and sound, with their leashes dragging behind them. They had had enough sense to follow along by themselves. Spot was there too, a short-legged hound dog with long floppy ears. Because of the mud, the children could not see what color he was. But neither could they see the color of the poodles. The four dogs were already friends, and, except for a slight difference in shape and size, they all looked exactly alike. Even Ruffles' blue ribbon had lost its clean color. When the dogs wagged their tails, muddy water flew in every direction.

At that moment they heard Mr. and Mrs. Brown beginning to call Sandra.

"Sandy darling! Time for lunch, Sandra! Where are you, angel?"

Kirby and Bitsy could not help laughing when they looked at Sandra, because she certainly did not look like an angel at that moment. Even her long yellow hair was caked with mud.

"Your mama told you to keep clean, Sandra," said Bitsy reproachfully.

There was only one good thing about it: neither Sandra nor the poodles looked bored. They had had a real good time.

"Coming, Mother and Daddy!" called Sandra. She sounded very cheerful and happy. And her smile was still nice and clean, if nothing else was.

10. Inside Miss Ferry's Cabin

The next thing the sitters had to do was to take the three poodles for a swim in the sea.

"We can't let Miss DeGree see them like this," Kirby said. In fact Kirby, Bitsy, Big and Spot all went in the water, too, clothes and all. It seemed the only way to get rid of the mud.

At the other end of the beach they could see Sandra bathing. Mr. and Mrs. Brown walked up and down on shore, clucking like hens who have hatched a duckling.

"Sandra darling, how *did* it happen?"

"Sandra, you're all right, aren't you, baby?"

"I'm fine," said Sandra happily. "I caught the alligator."

"Think of it!" Mr. and Mrs. Brown exclaimed together. "Our Sandra caught the alligator!"

Then Mrs. Brown said to Mr. Brown, "But darling, wasn't that dangerous?" And Mr. Brown said, "Merciful heavens! I'm afraid that it was."

Miss Ferry came by as the children were washing the poodles.

"Oh, Miss Ferry, please," called Kirby. "What do alligators eat?"

"Don't you know?" asked Miss Ferry in a reproachful voice.

"I'm afraid we don't," Kirby said. "Won't you please tell us?"

"Well, alligator food, of course!" Miss Ferry said impatiently.

"Could you—would you—do you have any in your hamper, please?"

"Please," said Bitsy.

"Please," said Big.

"I'll look and see," Miss Ferry said. "Come to my cabin as soon as you are through sitting. If I don't have any alligator food in my hamper, I can probably stir up a little something for you."

"And raspberry tarts, maybe?" Bitsy couldn't help adding.

"Good gracious, no!" cried Miss Ferry. "This is Tuesday. Tuesday is not the day for tarts. It's the day for ladyfingers."

"Mama doesn't let us lick our fingers," Bitsy said. Doubtless she had not understood Miss Ferry's words.

88

The waves, the palms and the weather vanes were all making their accustomed noises.

"Don't talk so much until you have cleaned the smudge off your nose, my dear child," Miss Ferry said. "I'll see you at my cabin as soon as you have delivered the dogs to their mistress."

When the children, clean and reasonably dry, presented themselves at Miss Ferry's door an hour later, she had a neat paper parcel marked ALLIGATOR FOOD all ready for them.

"What is it?" asked curious Bitsy.

"It's plainly marked," Miss Ferry said. "I hope that you have learned to read."

"Oh, yes," Bitsy said.

"And as to the ladyfingers," Miss Ferry added, "if you will be so kind as to step inside for a moment."

The children were pleased to step inside. The inside of Miss Ferry's cabin was very gay. It was almost completely lined with Miss Ferry's paintings. There was the one she had painted the first day, with the sheets and cabins and coco palms (naturally they did not look like any of those things, but Kirby remembered anyway). There was "Tribute to the Flag" with Marvello's handkerchiefs stuck among the ridges of sand. There was the one with Kirby's design of a coco palm tree painted black in the center. Also there were many, many more, all in the gayest of colors.

One small picture particularly interested Kirby because

it was done in pencil and it had a familiar Chinese look about it. It looked something like this:

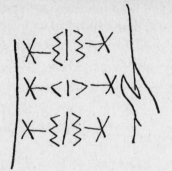

"Turn it around," Miss Ferry said. "You'll see that it is a picture of the motel and the palm trees reflected in the water."

"Why don't you turn it around when you hang it up, if it needs turning around?" asked Bitsy sensibly.

"Dear children, you ask so many questions," Miss Ferry said. "Of course, I hang it up the way it happened to come out when I drew it. But don't waste your time on that old thing. It's only a sketch that I tried to make many years ago. It didn't turn out too well."

"You made it with Uncle Hiram's pencil!" Kirby said accusingly.

"As a matter of fact, I did," replied Miss Ferry. "How did you know?"

"I tried to write my name with the pencil once," Kirby said. "The letters all turned out wrong."

"Well, what if I did use Hiram's pencil?" Miss Ferry asked. "An artist will try anything once. If it doesn't work out well, he can try something else. Here are your ladyfingers, children."

The ladyfingers were stuck together in pairs with a wonderful, fruity, nutty cream. They simply melted on the tongue.

Bitsy and Big rolled up their eyes in pleasure; but, even while Kirby ate his snack, he kept thinking about the mysterious pencil.

"Miss Ferry," he said, "did you know that Uncle Hiram's pencil is missing from his desk?"

"Dear boy," Miss Ferry said, "you should never try to speak with your mouth full." But then she added, "Missing? You say that Hiram's pencil has disappeared?"

"Yes, it has."

"That's odd. Perhaps Marvello borrowed it. I believe it was Marvello who gave it to Hiram in the first place."

"I don't know who took it," Kirby said. "But, whoever he was, he also rummaged all through the desk as if he was hunting for something."

"Ah!" Miss Ferry said. "No doubt he was hunting for a clue to the secret. Yes, that must have been it. A clue to the secret."

"Who would do a thing like that?" cried Bitsy. She had found her question-asking voice again, now that the snack was gone.

"It might be the gangsters, of course," Miss Ferry replied calmly.

"The gangsters?" repeated Kirby. "I thought I was the only one who knew they were gangsters."

"Poor dears!" Miss Ferry said, "it sticks out all over them."

"You mean the guns," said Kirby.

"I mean their whole appearance," Miss Ferry said. "It's unfortunate for them, but there you are. Some people never learn that it is really pleasanter and more fun to be good than to be bad."

"You think they might have taken the pencil?" Kirby asked. "Would that be a clue to the secret?"

"I don't think the pencil is the clue," Miss Ferry said. "But whoever was looking for the clue probably just saw the pencil and put it in his pocket."

"That was dishonest," Bitsy said.

"Of course it was," replied Miss Ferry. "Gangsters are usually dishonest, and stupid as well. In the old days villains were not only bad, but they had the sense to look bad too. You could tell them right off from other people. You didn't have to go around looking for gun bulges to tell the bad ones from the good."

"What were they like?" the children asked, "in the old days?"

"Well, of course, there were the ogres and the giants," Miss Ferry said. "They were terribly big and awkward, and most of them meant well but had turned bad because the smaller people couldn't bear to have them around. I think that Mr. Black is somewhat like a giant who has shrunk down and been led astray. Then, of course, there were the evil genii who lived in bottles and came billowing

92

out when you pulled the cork. They were long and thin and looked something like Mr. Locke."

Just then there came a knocking on Miss Ferry's door. "Come in," she said.

Jack Black stood on the threshold with a pair of scissors in his hand.

"Ah-ha!" Miss Ferry said, "speaking of ogres—"

"Excuse me, ma'am," he said, "but could I borrow some of your pink notepaper?"

"Why don't you go to the proprietor?" asked Miss Ferry. "He furnishes me with all the notepaper I need, which certainly isn't much."

"Daddy won't give Mr. Black any more notepaper until next week," said Bitsy. "He's used up all he's allowed on this week's rent."

"I see," said Miss Ferry. "And what do you do with so much pink notepaper, my bad man?"

Mr. Black's fat cheeks grew as pink as the pink notepaper.

"He makes beautiful doilies out of it," Bitsy said.

"Let's see you do it then," Miss Ferry said. "Here's a sheet of paper."

Mr. Black's eyes glittered when he saw the fresh piece of paper. He folded it from corner to corner in one direction, and then through the middle in the other direction, and then several times again. He snipped off the corners, and began to cut odd-shaped bits and pieces from the sides of the small folded triangle which remained after the folding. Snip, snip, snip, went his shears. Then with a triumphant air, he unfolded all the creases, and, presto! he had a beautiful round doily covered with a delightful pattern of butterflies and curlicue vines and leaves.

Miss Ferry clapped her hands. "That's wonderful!" she cried. "You are an artist, Mr. Black! I'll give you all my notepaper, and may I please keep this piece to work into my next picture?"

"Sure," said Mr. Black, blushing with pleasure. "I don't do nothing with them anyway. It's just for fun I make them, and to pass the time away."

"Well," said Miss Ferry, "you couldn't be better employed. Perhaps you and I can have an exhibit, Mr. Black. I will exhibit my pictures and you can exhibit your paper mats."

"Oh, ma'am, I'd like to," Jack Black said, "but Jimmy, my partner, he'd never let me do that. We got more serious business than this on our minds."

"What kind of business?" asked Bitsy.

"Oh—ah—well, fishing for one thing," Jack Black said.

94

"Now, Mr. Black," Miss Ferry cried, "confess that you have been rummaging in Hiram Stonecrop's desk."

"No! No!" muttered Mr. Black, backing quickly toward the door. "I didn't do that. Honest, I didn't. It was—"

Just then Mr. Locke's long, sour face appeared in the doorway behind Mr. Black.

"What are you doing here, Jack?" he said. "Come along now before you say anything which may be used against us."

"We were just partaking of some light refreshment, Mr. Locke," said Miss Ferry. "Will you and Mr. Black have some of my ladyfingers? They are very light."

"Light fingers, Jimmy," said Mr. Black eagerly. "That's just our specialty." He helped himself liberally to the plate of small delicious cakes. But Mr. Locke would not be lured into sociability. He hurried Mr. Black away without another word.

"Too bad," Miss Ferry said. "The long, thin one needed my hospitality more than the fat one. Jack Black is half reformed already. Now, if we could just save Jimmy Locke! I'm positive that he is a very bad influence on poor Mr. Black."

"They sure aren't up to any good," said Big. "Kirby, he knew it as soon as he saw 'em, didn't you, Kirby?"

"It's just because I watch TV," said Kirby modestly.

"Well, finish off the ladyfingers," said Miss Ferry, "and then don't forget the alligator."

The children *had* almost forgotten the alligator. They

95

really hated to leave Miss Ferry's cottage with its pictures and its snacks. But Miss Ferry was already putting on her floppy hat and preparing to go out painting.

" 'Bye now, children," she said. "See you later, alligator, as they say in Abyssinia."

11. Marvello's Troubles

Of course the alligator adored Miss Ferry's food. It came in pale green hunks and smelled something like fish and something like roast duck. The children were no wiser as to what alligators eat, when they got through feeding it to the creature, than they were before. But they could see by the pleasantness of the alligator's smile that he was satisfied.

"What shall we call him?" Bitsy asked.

"We ought to let Sandra name him," Kirby said, "because she caught him."

When they asked her, Sandra promptly named the alligator Pedro.

"Why?" asked Bitsy.

"I don't know why," Sandra said. "Do I have to have a reason?"

The other children thought it over, and they decided

that a reason for naming the alligator Pedro was not necessary.

"Now we have Pedro in this secret place," Sandra said, "it is too bad that we did not keep him a secret. We could play that he was the secret of your Uncle Hiram's motel, and that we were the only ones who knew it."

"Mr. Hiram, he sure had a secret long before we catched this alligator," Big said.

"Well, but we could play, couldn't we?" asked Sandra.

"Maybe we still can," Kirby said. "How many people know about Pedro?"

"I had to tell my daddy and mummy," said Sandra, "because they wanted to know how I got so dirty and why I was late for lunch. But I am sure that they won't tell anyone, because they are so busy lying on the beach getting tanned."

"Miss Ferry must know, because we asked her for alligator food, and she seems to be very smart," Kirby said. "Maybe we should go and ask her not to tell." He began to lick his lips as he thought of Miss Ferry. "Besides, Sandra has never had any snacks out of her hamper, have you, Sandra?"

"I really don't care about eating between meals," Sandra said.

"You will, if you have something out of Miss Ferry's hamper," said Bitsy. "This is Wednesday. What do you suppose she specializes in on Wednesday?"

"We might go find out," said Big.

The very mention of Miss Ferry's hamper made Kirby,

Big and Bitsy swallow in anticipation. However, when they reached Miss Ferry's cabin, they found it locked.

The Great Marvello was reclining in a deck chair in front of his cottage.

"She's gone out," he said to the children. "I saw her leave half an hour ago with her paints and easel and camp stool and hamper. I dare say she'll be gone all day."

The children went and stood around Marvello's chair.

"Mr. Marvello, this is Sandra Brown," said Kirby politely. "I guess you haven't met her before."

"It seems to me that I have," Marvello said. "Didn't I see you in Paris, my dear? Or was it in London?"

"No," Sandra said. "That couldn't have been me. I've never been to either of those places. I live in New York on Long Island. My parents and I are down here on a vacation to get a suntan."

"I've seen you somewhere," Marvello insisted. "Have you ever been to Athens? or Tokyo?"

Sandra shook her head. Her long blond hair floated about her shoulders in the breeze. She was smiling, and she looked very pretty.

Suddenly Marvello struck his hand against his forehead. "I have it!" he cried. "You remind me of the young lady I used to saw in two."

"Oh, no!" cried tenderhearted Bitsy.

"Don't worry, Bitsy," said Kirby. "The trick is done with mirrors, I believe, isn't it, Marvello?"

"My dear boy," said Marvello, "you must never disclose the secrets of our trade. It's one of a magician's first rules."

"I'm sorry, sir. Only I didn't want Bitsy to think that you really went around sawing girls in two."

"Do I honestly look like the girl you used to saw in two?" asked Sandra, pleased and interested.

"She was somewhat older than you, my dear, but still there is a strong resemblance."

"What happened to her?" Bitsy asked. "Did the saw slip? Or the mirrors get broken?"

"No," Marvello said. "It was nothing so simple as that. There used to be a very handsome young man in the audience. He kept turning up at every performance. He didn't understand about the mirrors, Kirby, and somehow he got the notion that the young lady needed rescuing. Actually, as you know, she wasn't ever in any real danger."

"So what happened?" asked Bitsy.

"Why, one day they ran away and got married. She left my act in midseason, and I was never able to get a replacement."

"Why not?" asked Bitsy. "Were all the other young ladies afraid you would really saw them in two?"

"I dare say they were," Marvello said. "Young ladies are often unduly fearful."

"*I* wouldn't be afraid," said Sandra scornfully.

Marvello looked at her thoughtfully. "You are very like her," he said. "Yes, very like."

"And did you have to give up the act then?" asked Kirby.

"That part of it, yes," replied Marvello. "I went on and finished the season as best I could without an assistant. But that was the beginning."

"The beginning of what?" asked Bitsy. "I should think it was the ending."

"Both, my dear child," said Marvello sadly. "It was the beginning of my professional decline; the end of my usefulness as a magician."

"Oh, don't say that, sir!" cried Kirby.

"Remember those shiny quarters you all found in our ears," reminded Big.

"The trouble is, I can't *count* on it," Marvello said. "Sometimes the magic works, and sometimes it doesn't. Now you see it, now you don't see it, as we say in the profession."

"Maybe if you were to practice a little," suggested

Sandra. "That's the way I get my music lesson. I practice scales and notes and—"

"Speaking of notes," Marvello said, "I see the postman coming up the road. Would you mind looking to see if he leaves anything for me? I'm rather expecting a communication from a fellow magician in Argentina."

Every day the postman drove up in a rattlety-bang old car and put the mail into a rural box held up by a figure of Uncle Sam which had been whittled by Mr. Carver and painted red, white and blue by Uncle Hiram.

Now the children ran to the mailbox in time to meet the postman. He handed the mail to Kirby, and it seemed that letters had come for almost everyone except Marvello.

"I'm sorry, sir," said Kirby.

"Never mind," the magician said sadly. "It's just part of my general decline that I no longer receive letters. Of course I could write them myself, and pluck them out of the air. But what's the use?"

"There's one here for Uncle Hiram," Kirby said. "That's odd."

"It must be from some former guest who doesn't know that Hiram has gone to his reward," said the magician. "Better take it to your father."

The children ran to take the letter to Mr. Mellen.

"It was mailed yesterday in the next town," said Mr. Mellen, looking at the postmark. "Please open it, Kirby, and read it aloud. I'm sure that Uncle Hiram would wish us to do so."

Kirby tore open the envelope and unfolded the single

102

sheet of paper. The message was short, but, before he had had time to read it, Kirby saw the name signed at the bottom of the page.

"Mr. Carver!" he shouted.

"Is he coming?" cried Bitsy.

"I sure do hope so!" cried Big.

"Who is Mr. Carver?" asked Sandra, but nobody paid any attention to her, because Kirby had started to read the letter.

Dear Hiram, the letter said, *I expect to arrive tomorrow about noon, walking as usual. I hope that you will find it convenient to put me up as you have so kindly done in the past.*

Faithfully yours,

Jonathan Carver

"Tomorrow noon?" said Mr. Mellen. "The letter was mailed yesterday in the next town. Good gracious! Mr. Carver is likely to arrive at any moment. Run, children, open up cabin number four, the Rooster, so that it will air. I'll tell Mother to put an extra plate on for luncheon. If the poor man's walking, he'll be hungry."

"I'll sweep the sand off his doorstep," said Big.

"I'll get him a pitcher of ice water," said Kirby.

"Let's us pick him a bouquet of flowers, Sandra," cried Bitsy.

Sandra didn't know what the commotion was all about, but she ran happily along with Bitsy to pick flowers. Something exciting always seemed to be happening at the Pink Motel.

103

12. Mr. Carver

At two minutes to twelve there was a cheerful sound of whistling, and a little, bandy-legged man was seen walking up the road toward the Pink Motel.

"It's him!" cried Big. "It's Mr. Carver, sure as you alive. Old Spot already seen him."

Sure enough, Big's dog Spot had met Mr. Carver down the road and was larruping along beside him. Several yellow butterflies were going along, too, circling cheerfully about Mr. Carver's battered hat.

Mr. Carver walked briskly, tootling to himself. On his back he carried a knapsack which bulged in an agreeably mysterious way. His clothes were old, but they were clean and neatly patched. Only his shoes were dusty.

When he saw the children running to meet him, Mr. Carver stopped whistling.

"God bless you all!" he said by way of greeting.

"Welcome to the Pink Motel, Mr. Carver," cried the children.

Right away Bitsy wanted to know, "When will you make a weather vane for our cabin, Mr. Carver?"

"Hush, Bitsy," Kirby said. "He doesn't even know yet that Uncle Hiram's gone."

"What?" said Mr. Carver. "Hiram no longer here?"

Talking fast and all at once, the four children began to tell Mr. Carver what had happened.

"He was very old—"

"And died. Our name is Mellen."

"But Miss Ferry's here—"

"And a magician, too—"

"And dogs and gangsters."

"Did he really have a secret?"

Mr. Carver was very easy to talk to. Bitsy and Sandra each took one of Mr. Carver's hands, and Big and Kirby larruped along beside with Spot. They continued to talk, everyone at the same time, telling Mr. Carver everything they could think of.

Mr. Carver kept smiling pleasantly, but suddenly Kirby noticed that one large tear had coursed down the side of his nose and hung like a pearl of dew on the end of it.

"Oh, I'm sorry, sir," Kirby said. "We've talked too much for you."

"Not too much," said Mr. Carver, "but a little too fast." He stopped in the middle of the roadway, and Sandra lent him a nice clean handkerchief from her pocket to wipe his tear away.

"I'm delighted that you are here," Mr. Carver said, "but first I must get used to the idea that poor, dear Hiram is gone. He was one of my very best friends. I wonder if he left me any message?"

"We don't know of any," Kirby said. "But perhaps you would like to look in Uncle Hiram's desk. We haven't cleaned it out yet, and there are more messages there than any of us have had time to read."

"Yes," Mr. Carver said. "If your father will allow me, I should be glad to look. There was a particular place where Hiram always left his messages for me."

Mr. Mellen did not object to letting Uncle Hiram's old friend look for a message in Uncle Hiram's office. Mrs. Mellen, to be sure, was a trifle disappointed by Mr. Carver's appearance.

"He's so plain," she whispered to her husband, "and patched. Not like those handsome gentlemen in pin-striped suits."

"But he's clean, my dear," said Mr. Mellen. "You always like things to be clean. And he looks honest."

Kirby opened Uncle Hiram's office and stood aside to let Mr. Carver go in. Mr. Carver sat for a moment in Uncle Hiram's swivel chair, but he did not open the desk. The children stood behind him, looking in from the doorway.

"How it all comes back to me!" Mr. Carver said. "Dear Hiram sitting here, laughing over the latest joke or nodding his head wisely over some old saying. Old sayings always fascinated him. 'The trouble is,' he used to say, 'that people get so tired of hearing them, they don't pay attention any more.' That was why he wrote the old sayings down on slips of pink paper. 'They deserve thought,' he used to say. 'If you stop to think each one out, it becomes a *new* saying.'"

"You may open the desk if you want to," Kirby said.

"No, thank you," Mr. Carver said. "I just want to sit here a moment to get the feel of it. Then I'll look in our special place and see if there is any message."

Presently Mr. Carver gave a long sigh, turned the swivel chair around three times and arose. He went to the row of coconut shells on the shelf which ran along the wall of the office. Kirby had been so busy with the contents of the desk that he had never gotten around to looking in the coconut shells.

"This was Hiram's filing cabinet," said Mr. Carver. "The last shell nearest the corner on the left was the one he kept for me."

"Oh, Mr. Carver," Kirby said, "maybe you can tell us what the labels on the coconuts mean. I never could figure them out. *Wint. 02*, for instance."

"Why, that means *Winter, 1902*," said Mr. Carver readily. "I never looked in that one, because I understand that 1902 was the winter when Hiram met Miss Kitty Sweetwater to whom he became engaged. Unfortunately Miss Kitty changed her mind and married someone else. But Hiram never forgot her, and I suspect that *Wint. 02* contains her letters."

"Oh!" the children said. "And *Hap. I*?"

"That contained Hiram's recipes for Happiness. He must have had a great many, because he was always so happy himself. Doubtless you will find coconuts marked *Hap. II, Hap. III*, and so forth, if you look around a little."

"And there is one that says something about an Imp taking a Bus," said Kirby, puzzled.

"Oh, you mean *Un. Imp. Bus.*," said Mr. Carver. "That's simply *Unimportant Business*. Someday it would be interesting to look into that one. So many things were important to Hiram, that it would be interesting to see if there was anything which he considered *un*important. Possibly we may find that one empty."

Now Mr. Carver came to the last coconut shell, and it was marked *Jon. Car.* He paused a moment thoughtfully before he turned the contents out into his hand. The coconut contained two slips of pink paper, a neatly laundered handkerchief and a small parcel.

"Ah, so this is where I lost my handkerchief!" exclaimed Mr. Carver. "Here you are, young lady, and thank you very much," he added as he restored Sandra's handkerchief to her, and put his own handkerchief into his pocket.

"What's in the parcel?" Bitsy asked.

"We'll read the pink slips first," said Mr. Carver gravely.

The first pink slip said:

> *A friend in need*
> *Is a friend indeed.*

"How true," said Mr. Carver. "Yes, it's one of those old familiar sayings which we need to re-examine for its real meaning. How often I have come to Hiram when I was in need, and he took this way of telling me that he was always my friend."

The other pink slip simply asked:

> *What shall we do about the coconuts?*

"Now this one," said Mr. Carver slowly, "I do not understand."

"I think I do," said Kirby. "There are so many coconuts and they are so hard to open. We don't know what to do with them, do we, Big?"

"No, we don't," said Big. "We pile 'em up in a pile, and we don't know what to do with 'em."

"I expect Uncle Hiram thought that you would know, Mr. Carver, because you are clever at making things."

"Hmm," murmured Mr. Carver thoughtfully. "Possibly you are right. I'll have to study on it, and see what comes to my mind."

"*When* are you going to open the parcel, Mr. Carver?" asked Bitsy, wriggling with curiosity.

"Right now," said Mr. Carver, breaking the string. "It's small, but it's heavy. I think I know by the feel—I hope—I certainly need a new one—"

Out of the small parcel came a new jackknife, all shiny with mother-of-pearl and steel. A beautiful jackknife! The sight of it made Kirby's eyes sparkle, for he was something of a whittler himself.

"Ah!" said Mr. Carver. "Just what I needed! Just exactly! The blade of my old knife is almost worn through, and I'm really afraid to cut hard wood with it, for fear it will break right off. This is indeed a cordial welcome to the Pink Motel."

"And now you can make a weather vane for *our* house, can't you, Mr. Carver?" cried Bitsy.

"I'll have to study on it for a while," said Mr. Carver, "but this will help. Yes, this will help."

"And now," said Kirby, "I expect you'd like to go to your cabin and freshen up for lunch. Mama has put on an extra place for you."

"Thank you! Thank you!" Mr. Carver said. "I see that you have inherited Hiram's kind heart as well as his motel."

"We picked flowers for you, Mr. Carver," said Bitsy and Sandra.

"We will carry your pack for you, Mr. Carver," cried Big and Kirby.

Mr. Carver had slipped the packsack off his shoulders, and now he let each boy take hold of a strap.

"Be careful with it," he said. "I've got a few little odds and ends in it that might be of interest to you, if they aren't broken."

"We're saving the Rooster cabin for you," all the children cried.

"Good!" said Mr. Carver. "That's the one I always occupy. When I was a boy about the age of Kirby and Big, I used to spend summers on my grandfather's farm. He had a big red barn and on the top of it was a weather vane carved like a rooster. I used to watch that rooster turning around and around to point the direction of the wind, and I said to myself, said I, 'When I'm grown to a man, I'll carve one like that!'"

"And so you did, didn't you?" asked Bitsy.

"Yes, I did, and I put it on top of the motel cabin where I happened to be staying at the time. Your Uncle Hiram came out of his office and looked at it. I scarcely knew Hiram then. It was my first time here. 'My good man,' said he, 'if you'll leave that weather vane there, I'll give you the use of the cabin free and for nothing. Do you know how to carve any other weather vanes?' So I told him I'd been studying on weather vanes all my life through. Then says he, 'Mr. Carver, come back every year, if you will, and make me a new weather vane. I'll never ask you a cent of rent.' "

"And you came six years, didn't you, Mr. Carver?" Bitsy asked.

"Yes," Mr. Carver said. "This is the seventh."

"And this year you'll carve one for *our* house, won't you?"

"Like I told you," Mr. Carver said, "I'm studying on it."

The four children followed him to the door of the Rooster cabin. Somehow they felt that they could not bear to part with him, even for a moment. They stood around his door, hoping that he would not close it.

He put his packsack on the bed and began to unpack. He did not have many clothes, but everything he had was clean. He had a comb and a toothbrush and a sponge in a waterproof bag. He had a small kit of tools and a very old and battered jackknife. The children could see why it was that he needed a new one.

After all these things had come out of his packsack, Mr. Carver began to take out the jumping jacks. He must have had fifteen or twenty of them, and he laid them out carefully in a row on his bed. These were what had made the mysterious bulges in his pack.

"You may come in now and take your pick," Mr. Carver said. The jumping jacks were small wooden figures painted like clowns. Their arms and legs were jointed, and each one was hung by a bit of string between two small sticks of wood. Whenever the bottoms of the sticks of

112

wood were pressed together, the jumping jack began to turn handsprings and somersaults. The children were delighted. Kirby chose a red one, Bitsy a blue one and Big a green one. Sandra took one that was as yellow as her yellow hair.

The children jumped, the jumping jacks jumped; and all of the weather vanes went whim! wham! slam! and bang! So Mr. Carver made himself at home in cabin number four, the Rooster.

With Mr. Carver around the place, everything seemed to run more smoothly. He tightened up the shutters so that they did not flap. With a little oil, he took the squeaks out of the door hinges. He stopped the leaky faucets, and improved the tuning of the radios.

"Dear me!" said Mrs. Mellen. "I like Mr. Carver better every day in spite of his patches. Even giving him free room and board, we shall be better off for having him with us."

When Miss Pamela DeGree's car refused to go, it was Mr. Carver who knew about cleaning the spark plugs and putting it in running order once more.

He added a few drops of something or other to the Browns' suntan lotion, and they found that they tanned much more quickly and could take a little time off for other diversions.

He caught a beautiful red snapper fish, and gave it to Mr. Black and Mr. Locke for their dinner. In spite of all the fishing they appeared to be doing, they had not yet tasted fish, and even their hard hearts were touched.

Mr. Carver showed Marvello how to tie a wonderful new slipknot which could be used in rope tricks and escapes.

"Where did you learn that, my good man?" asked the Great Marvello.

"I was a sailor once," replied Mr. Carver. "Sailors are always studying on the tying of knots, you know, just as boy scouts are. Well, we were becalmed for eight days once in the Sargasso Sea. The tying of this particular knot came to me then."

"I see," Marvello said.

"Sargasso Sea," corrected Bitsy.

The children wondered what Mr. Carver could possibly do for Miss Ferry, because she seemed capable of managing everything for herself. But one day, when Miss Ferry was having a difficult time with one of her pictures, Mr. Carver stood and looked at it critically for a while.

"May I take a hand?" he asked modestly.

"Take both hands, please," replied Miss Ferry graciously.

Mr. Carver went away, and returned some time later with three very ripe tomatoes. These he hurled rapidly at Miss Ferry's unfinished canvas. Each tomato left a vivid splotch of color which trickled down into a red fringe.

"Yes," Miss Ferry said. "I see now. That was all it needed. I shall call it 'Sunset on Three Beaches.' Thank you so much, my dear friend."

Mr. Carver was a very handy man to have around the place.

13. The Disarrangements Committee

"Isn't it about time to begin planning for the Concert?" Miss Ferry asked. She had stopped by the office of the Pink Motel on her way out to paint.

"Concert?" asked Kirby's father. "I don't know about any concert, Miss Ferry."

"I suppose you wouldn't know," she said. "But it was a regular thing with Hiram every season. He always organized a performance among his guests. Sometimes it was held on Christmas Eve, sometimes on New Year's Eve. It was not necessarily musical, although he called it a concert. You know, like the concerts they have on shipboard for the benefit of the Disabled Seamen."

"But we have no disabled seamen here," Mr. Mellen said, "at least we hope not."

"Hiram used to say that his Concerts were for the benefit of Humanity," Miss Ferry said, "and every year he gave the money that was collected to some worthy cause, such as the Salvation Army, or the Hungry Hungarians, or the Lonely Spinsters. One year he gave it to Big's father, because he needed to buy a new mule and he did not have the money."

"I know about it, Daddy!" cried Kirby eagerly. "There are lots of old concert programs in Uncle Hiram's desk. Marvello used to do tricks and Miss Ferry would give a chalk talk and lightning art exhibit, and Mr. Carver would give a 'Demonstration.' I don't know what that was."

"Mr. Carver's Demonstration varied from year to year," Miss Ferry said. "It was whatever he happened to be interested in at the time. Usually it was windmills and weather vanes, of course, but once it was glass blowing, and another time it was making boondoggles out of leather shoestrings. Why don't we ask Mr. Carver what he will do this year?"

"But really I don't believe that we shall have a concert this year," began Mr. Mellen.

"Oh, Daddy," Kirby cried, "let's do. Please. It will be fun."

"But who would organize it?"

"I'd be glad to organize it," Miss Ferry said. "I used to help Hiram. Only I must ask you to let Kirby and Bitsy help me on the Disarrangements Committee."

"We'd love to help!" Kirby and Bitsy cried.

"Why not?" said Miss Ferry. "And probably we'd better have Big and Sandra, too. Five heads are better than one."

116

"We'll go and get them right away."

"Good!" Miss Ferry said, "then we can call the Concert settled, can't we, Mr. Mellen? We'll go right ahead with it, and promise not to bother you any more than is necessary. Will that be all right?"

"Very well," Mr. Mellen said, "and I'm sure my wife and I will co-operate with you in any way we can. It's just that we have never done this sort of thing before. But if the responsibility is taken off our hands—"

"We'll attend to everything!" Miss Ferry said. She rubbed her nose and winked very pleasantly at Kirby and Bitsy. "The Disarrangements Committee will meet on the beach for lunch at twelve o'clock," she said to Mr. Mellen. "I hope that Kirby and Bitsy will be able to attend."

"If they won't discommode or bother you," said Mr. Mellen.

"Fine!" Miss Ferry said. "On the stroke of twelve, children, under the coco palm tree in front of my cabin. And don't forget to bring Big and Sandra."

"We'll be there," Kirby said. He and Bitsy were already beginning to swallow and lick their lips in anticipation of some new treat. And a concert! What fun! They ran to get Sandra and Big.

The four children were hanging about, pretending to be doing something else for fully half an hour before the stroke of twelve.

"When she says 'the stroke of twelve,' does she mean the first stroke or the last stroke?" Bitsy asked.

"We'll soon find out," Kirby said.

117

On the last stroke of twelve, the door of Miss Ferry's cabin flew open. Carrying her large straw hamper, Miss Ferry came briskly out.

"I see you are on time," she said, "and that is a virtue in any climate."

The children followed her down to the beach, eagerly wondering what came next. Probably they were thinking more about what was in Miss Ferry's hamper than they were about the Concert.

It took Miss Ferry some time to pick the right spot. She didn't like this one because of the sun; she didn't like that one because of the shade. Finally she found a spot under a coco palm tree that exactly suited her. It was half sun and half shade.

"So!" she said. "An artist learns to take a little trouble to get everything right. It pays in the long run." Now she opened her hamper and began to take things out.

At first there was a little difficulty with ants, palmetto bugs and crabs. They were all hungry, and they loved Miss Ferry so much that they came swarming around. But Miss Ferry was prepared in advance with packets of food marked *Crabs, Palmetto Bugs, Ants (large), Ants (small),* and *Ants (medium-sized)* which she tossed out to her friends.

"Now, run along, dears," she said, "and picnic by yourselves. This is a business meeting, and we must have our privacy." Soon the beach was cleared.

"They don't behave so well for us," Sandra said in surprise.

118

"You simply have to be firm with them," Miss Ferry said. "Kind but firm. There's no use spoiling them." Now she whisked out a white tablecloth and spread it on the sand under the palm tree. Next came blue willowware plates, knives, forks and spoons, cups and glasses, and pale blue napkins folded like cocked hats.

"Will you begin with dessert or vice versa?" she asked.

"We usually have the vice versa first," said Kirby, "but I think it might be more interesting the other way."

"What do you others say?" Miss Ferry asked politely.

"Dessert," the other children said.

"I like dessert first myself," Miss Ferry said. "It's the thing you enjoy most, but by the time you work your way to it through cauliflower, string beans, and Wiener schnitzel you have no room left to do it justice."

She opened the hamper again, and the children saw with pleasure that there were raspberry tarts, slices of melon, small frosted cakes, and chocolate puddings with whipped cream and a cherry on top.

They had a most delicious luncheon and they never did get around to the nutritious vegetable soup which is so good for growing children.

"Now this is all right for once," Miss Ferry said severely, when they were wiping the last bits of jam and cream from their faces with the pale blue napkins. "But don't expect your parents to start all your meals with dessert hereafter. They simply won't do it, and they're quite right, too. Children have to eat something besides dessert or they grow up to look like cream puffs. You wouldn't want to look like a cream puff, would you?"

Bitsy was just starting to say that she did not think she would mind, when up strolled the Great Marvello.

"I hope that I am not interrupting an important conference?" he said, looking hungrily at the hamper. It still seemed to be well stocked with food in spite of all they had eaten.

"This is a meeting of the Disarrangements Committee to plan the Concert," said Miss Ferry, "but, since you will undoubtedly be one of our best performers, we'll allow you to join us. Eh, children?"

"Yes! Yes!" the children agreed, making room for the magician beside them.

"I'm afraid I shall not be able to perform in the Concert this year," said Marvello sadly. "The magic is very dim, very dim. However, at this moment I am sure that I could make any number of those raspberry tarts disappear, Miss Ferry."

"Help yourself," Miss Ferry said. "But this is all nonsense about your not being able to perform. You must pull yourself together, Marvello."

"The thing that really started my decline," Marvello said, as tarts, cakes, puddings and slices of melon began disappearing down his throat in a truly magical way, "was the loss of my assistant. I was telling the children about it only the other day."

"Oh, you mean that young lady with the long blond hair that you used to saw in two. She was pretty, but I never thought her very smart," Miss Ferry said. "Now you take a girl like Sandra Brown. She has the long blond hair, she's reasonably smart, and, when she doesn't allow herself to get bored and sulky, she's quite pretty. How about Sandra Brown?"

Everybody looked at Sandra and for a moment she was too embarrassed to say anything.

"But, if you mean to saw Sandra in two, her parents would never let you," said Bitsy. "They're very particular about Sandra."

"I told you it isn't real, Bitsy," Kirby said.

"Well, I'm sure they'd make her wear her rubbers and spoil the look of things."

"Perhaps if we could get her parents to perform, too," Miss Ferry said, "they would be so busy thinking about themselves that they would forget her rubbers. Still, we had better let Sandra speak for herself. How about it, Sandra? Would you care to be Marvello's assistant for the Concert?"

"Well," said Sandra, "I think that Mr. Marvello should be the one to ask me."

"My dear young lady," cried Marvello gallantly, "I should be charmed! Simply charmed! Will you do me the honor of being my assistant on this great and glorious occasion?"

"I might," said Sandra. "Yes, I think I'd like to. The only thing is: will my parents let me?"

"What can your parents do, Sandra?" asked Miss Ferry. "I mean in the way of entertainment for the Concert?"

"They used to waltz together very beautifully," Sandra said. "Before they became so interested in getting perfectly tanned."

"The very thing!" cried Miss Ferry, clapping her hands in delight. "A waltz number would be charming. I'll ask them myself."

"The more I think about it," cried Marvello enthusiastically, as he made the last tart disappear, "the better I like the idea. I believe that Sandra will look very well when sawed in two. I almost feel the magic beginning to flow back into my finger tips. Miss Ferry, you have restored my courage. Thank you."

"Don't mention it," Miss Ferry said. "It was really the tarts and pudding that put new courage into you. And now, if you will go and practice your card tricks, Marvello, the Committee will get down to business."

14. Visit to the Alligator

For the next few days the children could think of nothing but plans for the Concert. Kirby even forgot to polish
up his J. Edgar Hoover G-Man badge or keep an eye on
the gangsters or worry about the pencil which was missing
from Uncle Hiram's desk.

"Now I want you children to find out what each one of
the guests can do in the way of entertainment," Miss Ferry
said. "That Miss Pamela DeGree now? Do her dogs perform?"

"They sit up and shake hands," said Kirby. "But they
are too well bred to be taught fancy tricks. They win blue
ribbons by just walking along on the ends of leashes with
their noses in the air."

"Let's have no noses in the air around here, neither in
girls nor in dogs," Miss Ferry said. "Every dog should
have an assortment of tricks. Poodles are smart, and they

123

can be taught a great deal in a short time. You children sit with them often, do you not?"

"Yes, we do."

"Fine!" Miss Ferry said. "I'll help you, and we'll see what we can do to train them."

"Maybe Miss DeGree won't like to have us teach them things."

"Go and ask her," Miss Ferry said. "I don't see how she can object. An educated dog is much more amusing to have around than an uneducated one. Dogs are like children, and I'm sure I never saw any child who was spoiled by learning spelling and arithmetic."

"What can the gangsters do in the Concert, Miss Ferry?" asked Big.

"I don't know," Miss Ferry said. "We'll have to ask them. Paper lace would be nice, but I suppose it will have to be something to do with guns. Perhaps one can shoot an apple off the other's head. That's a nice trick that originated in Switzerland, I believe, a long time ago when I was just a girl. But run along now, and find out about Miss DeGree's dogs."

Miss DeGree was busy shining her silver cups when the children knocked on her door. The three dogs were lying on the sofa looking very bored. But, as soon as they heard the children coming, they pricked up their ears and began to frisk and bark. With yelps of pleasure, Leo ran to Kirby, Ruffles ran to Bitsy, and Pantaloon ran back and forth between Sandra and Big.

"You surely have bewitched them," Miss DeGree said.

"All they do is yawn when I'm around. They even seem to be changing color since they have known you. I can't figure it out."

"Well, you see," Kirby said, "we didn't have time to tell you the other day, but they got muddy in the swamp and we had to wash them. Maybe we didn't get them as clean as they were before."

"Whatever were they doing in the swamp?" Miss De-Gree asked.

"Helping us catch an alligator," Kirby said. It popped out before he remembered that they had agreed to keep the alligator secret.

"It was only a very small one," Bitsy added. They looked at the dog's mistress anxiously. Was she going to object to alligator hunting?

"They had an awfully good time," Sandra said. "I did, too."

"But we won't do it again," Kirby added. "We are usually very careful with them."

"Because we know that they are very, very valuable," said Bitsy.

"Alligator hunting?" mused Miss DeGree. "That's a sport that I have never indulged in. I must try it sometime. Is alligator meat good to eat?"

"I don't think so," said Kirby. "Anyway we are getting fond of this one. We wouldn't like to eat him."

"I'd simply love to see him," Miss DeGree said. "Would you show him to me? Perhaps we could organize an alligator show and award prizes."

The children looked at each other doubtfully. But now that the secret was out, there seemed to be no reason why Miss DeGree should not look at the alligator if she wished to do so.

"It's quite a long way," Kirby said.

"I don't mind at all," said Miss DeGree. "I once won a prize for walking the mile in the shortest possible time."

As it was lunch time for the alligator anyway, the children led the way out to the palmetto thicket among the gumbo limbo trees where the old chest was hidden. Miss DeGree and the dogs followed along behind.

Kirby caught a couple of frogs on the way, and gave them to the alligator, together with his parcel from Miss Ferry. The alligator's smile seemed less dreadful to Kirby every day. Probably he was getting used to it.

Miss DeGree was most interested. "He would make a lovely handbag," she said. "But I suppose you are too fond of him for that?"

"Oh, yes," the children said.

"Not even a belt? or a pair of shoes?"

"We like him better alive," the children said.

126

When they closed the lid of the big brass-studded chest and started back to the motel, Kirby noticed a movement in a clump of palmettos some distance away.

"Don't look now," he said to the others, "but I believe that we are being watched."

Of course everybody turned and looked. How can you help doing so when someone says "Don't look"? They were just in time to see two men in plaid jackets emerging from the palmetto clump.

"Just as I suspected," said Kirby under his breath. "The gangsters!"

Mr. Black and Mr. Locke strolled along with the air of gentlemen out for a nature walk. Mr. Locke pointed to a mockingbird in a tree, and Mr. Black plucked a periwinkle and held it to his nose. But Kirby was not deceived. He knew that they had been watching him and the others as they stood around the chest.

"They are up to no good," said Kirby to himself. "I haven't been keeping an eye on them lately. I am afraid they are going to cause us trouble."

In a moment the children and Miss DeGree caught up with the two mysterious men.

"What a beautiful day!" said Mr. Locke in a cultured voice. "We have been taking a bird walk."

"Bird *walk?*" asked Mr. Black in surprise. "Them things don't walk. They fly."

Mr. Locke dug his elbow into Mr. Black's ribs. "*Bird* walk, Jack," he said. "You know, we were out walking to look at birds."

127

"Oh, *bird walk!*" Mr. Black said. "Sure. That was exactly what we was doing."

"Just minding our own business, we were," said Mr. Locke sweetly.

"And just what is your bus——?" began Kirby. But Bitsy suddenly remembered the Concert, and she said: "Now that you are all here together, we had better ask you what you will do in the Concert. We started out to ask Miss DeGree, but I guess we forgot."

"Concert?" inquired Miss DeGree and the two men. So the children had to explain all about the Concert, and how the proceeds were to go for the good of Humanity.

It seemed that Mr. Black and Mr. Locke had never even heard of the good of Humanity, and this part had to be explained to them several times.

"What it boils down to is, you expect to take in a lot of dough. Is that it?" asked Mr. Locke.

"We hope so," Kirby said.

"Ah-h-h!" said Mr. Locke and Mr. Black, looking at one another.

"But what will you do in the Concert?" Bitsy asked.

128

"We could sell tickets and take in the cash," suggested Mr. Locke.

"No," Sandra said. "You have to do something to entertain people. I am going to be sawed in two, and perhaps I shall also sing. Do you have any special talents?"

"Paper lace," suggested Mr. Black timidly, but Mr. Locke roared, "No! No, Jack. We can't have that!"

"Well, *honest*, Jimmy, I just thought—" began poor Mr. Black. But, of course, this caused Mr. Locke to roar "No! No!" again.

"What *will* you do then?" asked Bitsy.

"We could do our knife-throwing trick, Jack," Mr. Locke said. Mr. Black seemed very doubtful about this.

"I got a nick in the ear, the last time you threw knives at me," he said. "Still if it's for this good of Humanity thing, I guess I could let you try again."

"That sounds very exciting," said Miss DeGree. "I might put on a weight-lifting exhibition or I might do a drill with Indian clubs. There are quite a number of things I could do."

"And how about the dogs?" asked Sandra.

"We might exhibit their silver cups and blue ribbons," Miss DeGree said. "Silver cups?" inquired Mr. Locke.

"Oh, yes," Miss DeGree said, "I have ever so many. These are very, very valuable dogs, Mr. Locke."

"*These* dogs?" asked Mr. Black in surprise. "You say they're worth a lot?"

"Remember, Jack? The little girl told us that the very first day."

129

"We almost forgot," said Mr. Black. "So the pooches are valuable?"

"Indeed they are," said Miss DeGree proudly.

"Oh, Miss DeGree," cried Bitsy eagerly, "would you let us teach the dogs some tricks? We want them to perform in the Concert, too."

"I see no objection to letting you try," Miss Degree said. "They never do anything but yawn for me."

"Bow!"

"Wow!"

"Yap!" cried the three dogs eagerly. It seemed as if they had understood every word.

The children were so pleased at the idea of teaching the dogs tricks, that they scarcely noticed the interested look which the two men gave to the three very valuable dogs. Even Kirby failed to notice this because he was thinking: I'll teach Leo to roll over and beg and say his prayers—

"Very, very valuable," Mr. Locke was murmuring as the two men walked away, and Mr. Black mused, "Silver cups! Oh, boy!"

15. Poodle Tricks

When the children went to look for Mr. Carver, they found him standing beside the pile of coconuts which Kirby and Big had gathered together.

"Coconuts," Mr. Carver mused. "What shall we do about the coconuts?"

"Mr. Carver," the children cried, "we are helping Miss Ferry make plans for the Concert. You will give a Demonstration, won't you?"

"You are in all of the old Concert programs, Mr. Carver," Kirby said.

"What will you do?" asked Bitsy.

Mr. Carver sighed. "My ideas are rather vague this year. I have been standing here for half an hour, looking at these coconuts, and not a single idea has come into my head. I must be getting old. I guess you'll have to excuse me from taking part in the Concert this year."

"Oh, Mr. Carver!" the children cried. "You *must* be in the Concert."

"Of course," Mr. Carver said, "I could do some of the same old things—windmills, jumping jacks, weather vanes. But the people who come to these concerts year after year have seen me do all those."

"Study hard, Mr. Carver," urged the children.

"Marvello thought that he had lost his magic," Sandra said, "but I am going to be his assistant, and now the magic seems to be coming back to him."

"Perhaps if I had an assistant," murmured Mr. Carver thoughtfully.

"I will be your assistant, Mr. Carver," Bitsy said. "The only thing we need is to find something to demonstrate."

"It's these coconuts that bother me," Mr. Carver said. "If I could think of a use for them! You have tried eating them, I suppose?"

"Oh, yes," Kirby said. "We tried that right away, and we do eat a good many. But they are very hard to open, and after a while we get tired of eating coconut."

"Even coconut cake," added Bitsy.

"And Mr. Stonecrop, he ask you, 'What shall we do about the coconuts?'" put in Big.

"I know," said Mr. Carver sadly. "*Waste not, want not,* Hiram used to say, and also, *There's a use for everything, if you just think of it.*"

"Yes," Kirby said. "I found both of those things written down on pieces of pink paper in his desk."

132

"Uncle Hiram used empty coconut shells to keep things in," said Bitsy. "Maybe we could put up a few more."

"But there isn't room for any more coconut shells on Uncle Hiram's shelves," Kirby said.

"It ought to be something *different*," said Sandra. Since she had got the idea from Bitsy, Sandra wanted everything to be as different from everything else as possible.

"There's only one thing I keep seeing when I look at these coconuts," said Mr. Carver slowly. "But I fear it wouldn't lead to anything."

"What is it?" Bitsy asked. "Maybe we could help you, if we knew what it is."

"Well," Mr. Carver said, "the odd thing is, I see faces in them. I'll have to study this a little bit. When I see a block of wood, I know right away what it has in it. I see a long, narrow piece of wood, and I say to myself, 'It's got a giraffe in it,' and, sure as shootin', when I take my knife and whittle it, out comes the giraffe. Now all of a sudden I see heads and faces in these coconuts. Funny thing! I never noticed this before."

Suddenly a light began to glow in Mr. Carver's eyes. He took his new knife out of his pocket and began to carve and shape the outside husk of the coconut. He cut eyes and mouth and left a large piece sticking out for a nose. He scraped the chin, and in a moment the fibers of the coconut grew rough and hairy like a beard.

"What do you think of it?" Mr. Carver asked.

"It's wonderful!" the children cried.

133

"But what is it good for?" Mr. Carver sighed. "A weather vane is good for something. It tells the way the wind blows."

"Why, this is like Miss Ferry's pictures and Mr. Black's paper lace," said Bitsy. "It's to look at and enjoy."

"You could make many different kinds of faces," Sandra said.

"And paint them," said Big.

"Paint them!" exclaimed Mr. Carver. "So I could. So I could! Just a few touches of color here and there, and we'll have an amusing face."

"Oh, Mr. Carver," cried Bitsy, "that can be your Demonstration for the Concert. You can make different kinds of faces on all the coconuts; and I'll stand by and hand the coconuts to you. Maybe I can even paint some."

134

"Well, well!" Mr. Carver said. "It's quite an idea. Do you think anyone would be interested?"

"We would!" the children cried. "And Uncle Hiram would have been pleased, too."

"Well, well, well!" said Mr. Carver happily. "Now that this is settled, we shall have to think about the other details of the Concert. There are programs to print—"

"And tickets," said Kirby.

"That's right. Hiram had an old typewriter somewhere about the place. Does anyone know how to operate it?"

"I'll bet Miss DeGree does," Bitsy said. "Maybe she would type the programs while we are training her dogs."

"And, of course, there will be the stage to build," said Mr. Carver, "and the folding chairs to borrow from the Ladies' Uplift Society."

"Where do you put the stage?" asked Kirby.

"Right in front of the Pink Motel where people usually park their cars," said Mr. Carver. "And then, of course, there will be the lights to wire, because the Concert is always held in the evening; and the microphones to install."

"Can you do all of those things, Mr. Carver?"

"I used to help Hiram to do them, so I'm sure I can. Perhaps your father will help me, and I am sure that Miss Ferry and Marvello will lend their support. Maybe I could get those two gentlemen in number five to help me with the heaving and the hauling. They look right strong in the muscles, if just a trifle weak in the heads."

"I wouldn't count too much on them," said Kirby. "I think their intentions are pretty bad."

135

"Well," said Mr. Carver, "Hiram used to say *Satan finds work for idle hands to do.* Maybe, if we were to keep their hands busy, heaving and hauling, they wouldn't find the time for badness."

"It's an idea. Maybe it's worth trying."

But, unfortunately, every time that the two gangsters were wanted for some good and useful work, no one could find them. Sometimes they were out in a boat, poking around with sticks in shallow water; sometimes they were skulking through the palmetto thickets. When any honest labor was required of them, they were sure to be absent.

Sometimes in the evening the children saw the two men practicing knife-throwing or shooting at a target.

"They are getting ready for the Concert anyway," said Bitsy, "even if they don't help Mr. Carver."

"They are very, very quick on the draw, I notice," said Kirby. "I better practice up a little bit on that myself. I haven't tried it for a long time."

Now the children became absorbed in the delightful task of teaching Miss DeGree's poodles to do tricks.

Although Miss Ferry had promised to help them, she was very much taken up with the task of providing curtains for the Concert stage. Somewhere in one of Hiram's sheds she had found an old spinning wheel and a loom for weaving, and she was very busy spinning and weaving yards and yards of pale blue gauze.

"You'll have to train the dogs yourselves, my dears," she said. "Just look in my hamper, and you will find a little something to assist you."

136

The four children eagerly crowded around the hamper, scarcely daring to touch it. Finally Bitsy took hold of the cover and raised it slowly. Everybody was swallowing and dreaming of tarts, puddings, cakes and confections; but, when the lid of the hamper was lifted, they saw that there was absolutely nothing inside except a small paper parcel marked *Poodles*.

"What day is this?" asked Bitsy.

"Thursday," said Miss Ferry. "Why did you ask, dear child?"

"I just wondered," said Bitsy.

"Well, don't give up hope," Miss Ferry said. "I've been extremely busy with this tiresome curtain, but I might be induced to stir up something later."

"We wouldn't want to bother you," the children said politely.

"Well, read the directions on the poodle package," Miss Ferry said. "As Hiram used to say so often, *While there's life there's hope*. Now run along, for goodness sake."

When the children reached cabin number two, the Prancing Horse, they found the poodles eagerly waiting for them.

"Remember to be kind to them," Miss DeGree said, "and that they are very, very valuable."

"We will," Kirby promised.

"Ta-ta, then," Miss DeGree said. "I'm off to help Mr. Carver with the programs."

The dogs began to bark and dance around the children, sniffing the parcel marked *Poodles*.

"Read the directions, Kirby," Sandra said.

Kirby unfolded the slip of paper which was stuck under the string of the parcel, and read:

Directions: Whenever a poodle has learned a trick, he may be rewarded with one of these snacks.

The poodles sat quietly as if they were listening while Kirby read. They looked at one another with their tongues hanging out. It seemed as if they were laughing.

"Sure looks like they had a joke on us," said Big.

Suddenly Leo began to roll over, Pantaloon lay down and began to play dead, and Ruffles stood on her hind legs and began to waltz.

"Why, they already know some tricks!" cried Kirby in surprise.

"Miss DeGree didn't tell us!" said Sandra.

"Why not?" wondered Bitsy.

"Maybe she didn't know," said Big.

After they had done their tricks the three poodles crowded around Kirby and looked at the parcel from Miss Ferry's hamper. They began to whine. They sat up on their hind legs and begged. There was nothing to do but reward them handsomely with the small brown nubbins of hard-cooked liver from the parcel.

From then on it was a very simple matter for the children to teach a number of additional tricks to these intelligent animals. Kirby taught Leo to jump through an old hula hoop. Sandra taught Pantaloon to climb a ladder. Bitsy taught Ruffles to walk on her front feet with her hind legs in the air. And Big taught all of the dogs to

138

sneeze. The poodles were very glad to learn these new things, because every effort was rewarded with a snack.

It was a most successful training period, but presently the children found that they were more tired than the poodles. Naturally the poodles had been refreshed with the delightful snacks. The poor children had had nothing.

When all of the poodle snacks were gone, the children sat down to rest. Sandra happened to pick up the slip of paper on which were written the *Directions*. She looked at it curiously at first, and then with surprise.

"Why, Kirby," she said, "you didn't read these directions right."

"Oh, yes, I did," said Kirby.

"Oh, no, you didn't," Sandra said. "It says here:

Directions: Whenever a child has taught a trick to a poodle, he or she may he rewarded by applying to Miss Ferry."

The children crowded around to look.

"I'm sure it didn't say all that before," said Kirby.

"But it must have. You must have been mistaken the first time."

"How could I be?"

"Well, use your eyes, Kirby. You see what it says now."

"Yes," Kirby said, "I see. I see—"

"What are we waiting for?" asked Bitsy sensibly.

"Let's go!" cried Big.

It turned out that on Thursday there were small pastries filled with custard and cream and dipped in melted chocolate. There were a lot of them.

16. "Help! Help!"

Early in the morning, on the day of the Concert, Miss DeGree took her three poodles to the Canine Beauty Salon to have them freshly clipped and combed. The Canine Beauty Operator put silver nail polish on all of their toenails. More exquisite animals were never seen at the Pink Motel nor anywhere else in the world, the children felt. Everybody stood around, when the poodles returned to the motel, and gazed at them admiringly.

"They really look as very, very valuable as you have always said they were, Miss DeGree," said Bitsy. The others all agreed with her.

Even Mr. Black and Mr. Locke came to look at the beautiful poodles.

"Chee!" murmured Mr. Black. "Silver toenails!" The eyes of Mr. Locke popped out with surprise, but he did not say a word.

Miss DeGree was very much flattered by all of this attention, but she did not like to show it. So she put on a businesslike air and began to bustle about. "Now," said she, "I shall shut the little angels in my cabin where they can rest and keep nice and clean and beautiful. And I myself shall go and put the finishing touches on the programs for the Concert."

It was a very busy day for everyone—everyone except the gangsters, of course, for they went out in their boat as usual and left the hard work to be done by others.

"Don't forget to come back for the Concert," called Bitsy.

"We won't," they said.

The children ran up and down all day, doing errands and attending to a dozen different jobs. Miss DeGree was busy with the programs, and Mr. Carver was pounding away at the platform for the stage. Mrs. Mellen was busy making costumes, and Mr. Mellen was arranging lights and setting up chairs. In fact, at this point, Mr. and Mrs. Mellen were just as excited about the Concert as everybody else.

The last anyone had seen of Marvello, he was in his cabin busily picking cards, flags, coins and other small articles out of thin air. "I can't fail now," he was muttering to himself. "I can't let my assistant down by flubbing any of my tricks." Mr. and Mrs. Brown were still on the beach, but they were not idle. They were busily weaving garlands of greenery to decorate the stage.

Miss Ferry was in her cabin, running up curtains of the

blue gauze on an old sewing machine of Hiram's. The sewing machine made a buzzing, creaking noise, which blended pleasantly with Mr. Carver's hammering. Of course the palm leaves rattled, the waves roared, and all of the weather vanes went whiz! bang! slam! and whirr!

"Oh, isn't it delightful?" Bitsy cried, and all of the children agreed that it was.

Miss DeGree finished the last of the programs along in the afternoon. She put them in a neat pile, all ready for the ushers to hand out in the evening.

"Now I must air my dogs," she said.

"Can't we do that for you?" asked the children.

"Not this time, thank you," Miss DeGree said. "They like to go with you, as you know, but sometimes they get dirty. Today nothing must happen to spoil their beautiful appearance."

Presently the children saw her set out with Leo and Pantaloon on their leashes.

"Ruffles didn't go," said Bitsy.

"She was probably asleep," Kirby said.

"Give me a heave-ho with these curtain rods, please," called Mr. Carver.

After that, there was a great fuss of putting up curtain rods and hanging yards of blue gauze. A carpet had to be laid on the plank stage. Potted palms had to be fetched, and more folding chairs carried and set in place. Everybody rushed about, shouting directions and advice. Sometimes they were all gathered about the stage; sometimes, for a few moments, everybody would vanish on a different errand, and the whole place would seem to be deserted.

At last the arrangements were almost complete, and the children stood admiring their handiwork.

"Who'd ever think it?" Kirby cried. "It's like a theater instead of a parking place." They were tired, but they all felt satisfied and happy.

At this moment it did not seem that anything could possibly happen to dampen their spirits. Even when Mrs. Mellen suggested that the children should take naps to prepare them for staying up late, the children were quite willing to do so. Without making the slightest fuss, they cast a last admiring look at the Concert stage, and started to go away to their beds.

But suddenly, in the midst of the pleasant and familiar sounds of wave and palm and weather vane, there came another sound that chilled the heart of everyone who heard it. It was a voice crying for help. For an instant everyone froze in his tracks to listen.

"Help! Help!" a voice kept crying. The sound came from the Prancing Horse cabin where Miss DeGree lived with her poodles. As the children ran toward it, they met Miss DeGree coming out. She was crying and wringing her hands, and, at first, she could say nothing but "Help!"

Two of the poodles ran anxiously beside her. They were Leo and Pantaloon.

"What is the matter?" asked Kirby and Big and Sandra.

"Where is Ruffles?" asked Bitsy.

At last Miss DeGree found words. "Oh, Ruffles is gone!" she cried. "I stepped out for a short time and left Ruffles alone in the cabin. The other two dogs came with me, but Ruffles was sleeping and didn't want to come. When we returned, the cabin was empty. Ruffles had disappeared."

"She's probably hiding under the bed," said Kirby.

"Oh, no, she isn't," Miss DeGree cried. "I've looked and I've looked. And all the silver cups are gone, too. The blue ribbons are there, but the silver cups are gone. My most valuable dog and all the silver cups. They've disappeared as if by magic."

"Magic?" Kirby said. Instantly the word made him think of the magician. But surely the great Marvello would never play a trick like this.

Miss DeGree's cries for help had caused other people to come running to see what was the matter. Mr. Carver and Kirby's father and mother and Miss Ferry arrived first, and then came Marvello and Mr. and Mrs. Brown.

Poor Miss DeGree had to keep repeating her story to each new arrival. "I've been robbed." Miss DeGree cried. "Oh, heavens! I've been robbed!"

144

"This is dreadful!" Kirby's father said. "Robbers in our motel! We certainly can't have that. It's most embarrassing."

"It can't be so!" cried Kirby's mother. "It simply can't be so!"

"But it is so!" sobbed Miss DeGree. "I wish I had never stopped at this terribly pink motel."

"If only we had got around to painting it a different color," Mr. Mellen said, "we shouldn't have had such odd guests."

"Odd!" cried Mrs. Brown to Mr. Brown. "Darling, this churlish fellow is calling us odd!"

"Yes," replied Mr. Brown, "and think of this, my dear: a dog has been kidnaped! It might have been our Sandra."

"Oh, Daddy," Sandra said, "I'm fine. Nothing has happened to me."

"It's probably the magician," said Mrs. Brown. "He plans to saw our child in two. Goodness knows what else he might stoop to!"

"So the doggie just disappeared into thin air, as it were," remarked Marvello thoughtfully. "Now you see her, now you don't see her. It looks like a magician's work to me."

"Oh, it does, does it?" cried Miss DeGree angrily. "Maybe you *are* the one who did it, Mr. Marvello?"

"I suspect Mr. Carver," Mrs. Mellen said. "He seems very nice, but, after all, he is quite poor enough to need to steal, and nobody knows a thing about him."

"Mama!" cried Bitsy reproachfully. "Mr. Carver is our friend."

145

But the grown-up people were far too excited to listen to the children.

"Or how about Miss Ferry?" cried Miss DeGree. "She makes the oddest things happen. I declare, I don't know who is my friend any more."

"I suspect those two men who go out fishing and never catch any fish!" cried Mr. Carver.

"The gangsters!" exclaimed Miss Ferry.

"Gangsters?" shrieked Mrs. Brown. "Do you mean to say that there are gangsters in this motel?"

"Didn't you *know?*" asked Mr. Carver.

"Where are they now?" demanded Miss DeGree. "They aren't here, are they?"

"They went out in a boat this morning, the same as always," said Big.

"Could they have come back without being seen?"

Nobody knew, but it seemed quite possible. There had been so much confusion.

"They might be the ones. Yes, I'm sure they *are* the ones," Miss DeGree cried. "I told them about my silver cups and how valuable my dogs were. They're very suspicious-looking characters!"

"We must be calm," Miss Ferry said. "We'll never find out if we allow ourselves to become excited."

"It's easy enough for *you* to be calm," sobbed Miss DeGree. "It wasn't *your* pet that was stolen."

"This is terrible!" said Mr. Brown. "Gangsters! Dognapers! We had better pack and leave at once."

"Oh, no!" cried Sandra. "Please, we can't leave before

146

the Concert. Mother! Daddy! Things are just beginning to get interesting."

"It looks very suspicious if anyone wishes to leave now," cried Miss DeGree. "Perhaps Mr. and Mrs. Brown know something about all this. Perhaps *they* are the guilty ones."

"Dear me, no!" cried the Browns, "but we'll certainly stay if you are going to suspect us for leaving. It is really very horrid of you to be so suspicious."

"Well, it is horrid to have my precious dog stolen. Yes, and all my silver cups. Any one of you might be guilty."

Kirby stood silent through all of this confusion. He was amazed to see his good friends transformed into shouting, quarreling strangers, suspecting each other and calling each other names. This was the first time that he had seen sensible people lose their heads in a moment of excitement. Now he realized how easily such a thing can happen.

As he was wondering how he could stop them, he heard Miss Ferry's voice.

"Come, come!" she cried. "Stop and think a moment. What would Hiram have done under these circumstances?"

"Hiram!" everybody exclaimed. For a moment they stopped quarreling and suspecting each other to think calmly about old Hiram Stonecrop.

"I wish Hiram were here," remarked Marvello, and Mr. Carver said, "He might have left a message."

"Kirby," said Mr. Mellen, "perhaps you had better go and look into Uncle Hiram's desk. You may find something that will enlighten us."

147

Kirby was delighted to escape to the peace and quiet of Hiram's office. The usual smell of musty contentment rose up around him when he opened the desk. Not knowing exactly what he was looking for, Kirby rummaged hastily among the papers. He found one that said *Stollen,* but it turned out to be a recipe for coffee cake instead of a way to catch robbers.

Another pink slip said, *Who steals my purse, steals trash.* But that did not seem to apply to this particular case, for Ruffles was certainly not *trash,* and Miss DeGree would certainly not wish anyone to say so.

Two other slips seemed helpful. One said, *Do It Yourself,* and the other said,

> *Birdies in their nest agree,*
> *And so, kind friends, why cannot we?*

Kirby put the *Do It Yourself* slip in his pocket, and ran back to read the other slip aloud to his friends. They listened politely, but no one seemed impressed.

Miss DeGree stopped weeping for a moment to say, "I don't see how that can help us."

"The question is dogs, not birdies," objected Marvello.

"But don't you see," said Kirby, "if we would all stop quarreling and work together we might be able to solve this mystery? Before we begin to suspect each other, we should look for clues."

"Well spoken, Kirby," said Miss Ferry. "Here is a boy with a bit of sense in his head. He wears the J. Edgar

148

Hoover Junior G-Man badge. I make a motion that we put him in charge of this case."

"An excellent idea," said Mr. Carver. "I second the motion."

The others all agreed to let Kirby take charge.

"First of all," said Kirby, "we must search Miss De-Gree's cabin. We must be very careful not to touch anything, because we don't want to get our fingerprints mixed up with those of the criminals'."

"Now we're going to get a little bit of action," remarked Miss Ferry approvingly.

17. An Oddly Written Note

They all crowded into Miss DeGree's cabin and began to look under the bed, in the closet, under the table and the chest of drawers, and behind the bathroom door. They turned the pictures around and looked at the backs of them. Marvello got out a magnifying glass and Miss Ferry put on her spectacles. No one found any clues.

"There's nothing here," everybody said.

"Don't see a thing," said Big.

"The place is empty," said Sandra.

"Poor, dear darling Ruffles!" mourned Bitsy.

Kirby stood still in the middle of the floor and began to think.

"We have looked in all the difficult places first," he said, "but how about the easy ones?"

"The easy ones?" everybody repeated in surprise.

"Yes," Kirby said. He stood still and looked all around

him, and suddenly he saw something that nobody had
noticed because it was in plain sight. In the middle of the
bathroom mirror, fastened with Scotch tape, was a piece
of paper. It bore the following message:

> ξ°224.ΔᴱGNᴇ ≗7ʌoυ ʌʌʟυℲ ʌoυʌ
> 4oo7H ʟᴇʌʌᴇ ᵗᵉ1ooo ≗z Ŧᴇ <Hᴇzʟ
> 8ᴇH°ᴺᴅ Ŧᴇ ξ°ʟᴇʟ oz Ŧᴇ zᴅᴎoᴋᴇ
> o7 12 ʌ7ʟᴇᴺ Ŧᴇ coᴎcᴇᴧʟ
> ʌoυᴺz ᴍ°ʟH ʟoʌᴇ
> Ŧᴇ Δ0Gᴎʌ44ᴇᴎz.
> 4.z. Ŧᴇ ʟoʌᴇ ≗z oᴎʟʌ ≗7 ʌoυ
> o8ᴇʌ oᴎᴅᴇᴎz ʌᴎφᴅo ᴎoʟ
> ʟᴎʌ ʌᴎʌ ʟᴎ°7ᴋz.

"It's written in Chinese," Mr. Brown said.

"A ransom note!" sobbed Miss DeGree.

"It's in code," said Mr. Mellen. "How can we tell what
it says?"

"I think that I can read it," Kirby said calmly. "Anyway I can tell you how it was written."

"How?" everybody asked—everybody, that is, except
Miss Ferry. She smiled at Kirby and nodded her head
knowingly.

"It was written with a pencil which has a crooked handle
on the end where the eraser ought to be," Kirby said.

"Why, that was Hiram's pencil!" cried Marvello. "I gave it to him myself. It was a small gift which I purchased for him in a bazaar in Hong Kong."

"Yes," said Kirby, "and it has been missing from Uncle Hiram's desk for several days—ever since his desk was searched."

"But what does the message say?" asked Miss DeGree.

"It says: *Miss P. DeGree*," read Kirby slowly, "*If you value your pooch, leave $1000 in the chest behind the motel on the stroke of 12 after the Concert. Yours with love, The Dognapers. P.S. The love is only if you obey orders and do not try any tricks.*"

"Oh!" cried Miss DeGree, sinking into a chair. "I feel very faint. Indeed, I do!" The two remaining poodles jumped into her lap and tried to lick her cheeks. Perhaps this revived her, for Miss DeGree did not faint.

After they found the mysterious ransom note, the people from the Pink Motel went in every direction hunting for the lost poodle. They went up and down the roads and into the swamp and along the canal.

Big let his dog Spot smell one of the doll dresses Ruffles had worn, and Spot set off bravely, sniff-sniffing the ground. It looked as if he had found the trail. But presently the trail led him down to the edge of the sea. He ran back and forth, sniffing until he became quite confused, and finally he ended by chasing around and around after his own tail.

Poor Miss DeGree began to cry again. "Perhaps Ruffles has been drowned," she sobbed. "And, even if she is alive,

152

how am I ever going to gather together a thousand dollars? I'm really not rich. All I had was my valuable dogs and my silver cups."

"We must all help you," Miss Ferry said. "Perhaps I can sell a picture."

"We'll take up a collection," said Mr. and Mrs. Brown.

"Perhaps I can sell the rest of my jumping jacks," said Mr. Carver.

"Look!" cried Marvello. "Here is a quarter sticking out of your ear, Miss DeGree."

"We could lend you the money we take in at the Concert," said Mr. Mellen, "and you could pay it back to Humanity when you were in funds again."

"Oh, you are very kind!" cried Miss DeGree. "I see that you are true friends after all. Why did I ever suspect any of you?"

Kirby was glad that the ransom money would be taken care of. But he felt that it would be even better if the dognapers could be caught before the money had to be paid.

The grown people were all upset and excited, and Kirby saw that he would certainly have to handle the case of the missing poodle himself. He felt that he could trust Bitsy and Big and Sandra, because they had been friends of Miss DeGree's dogs and would not wish to kidnap one of them for ransom. He knew that Miss DeGree herself was innocent, but she was so nervous and upset that she was of very little help to him. Mr. and Mrs. Mellen were completely confused and bothered by the whole affair, and Mr. and Mrs. Brown could think of only one thing: It might have been Sandra who was kidnaped instead of Ruffles. Mr. Carver, in spite of his patches, seemed to be out of it, but two things in the ransom note bothered Kirby. There was the word *tricks* which seemed to suggest Marvello. And there were the words *on the stroke of 12* which suggested Miss Ferry.

Also there was the fact that Miss Ferry had made a sketch with Hiram's pencil. She said that she had made it a long time ago, and Kirby had never known her to tell an untruth. Still, as any detective knows, the investigator must not overlook any possible clues.

Big suspected the alligator, because of the fact that the thousand dollars was to be put into the chest.

"Alligators," he said, "is very mean and ornery critters. They smile, but they don't smile pleasant."

"But how could an alligator write a note?" Sandra asked.

"And what would it do with the money?" asked Bitsy.

"It *is* strange that the money is to be put into the old chest," Kirby said. "Who, besides ourselves and the alligator, knows about the chest?"

"Miss DeGree does," said Bitsy.

"You don't suppose she wrote the note herself, surely?" asked Sandra.

"Oh, I don't think so!" Kirby said. "Your parents know, don't they, Sandra?"

"I told them about the alligator," Sandra said, "but I am sure I didn't mention the chest. Even if I had, they wouldn't know where to find it."

"But remember the day we met Mr. Black and Mr. Locke taking their bird walk," said Bitsy. "I don't think they saw the alligator, but they must have caught a glimpse of the chest."

"Yes," Kirby said, "everything comes back to them. I suspect them the most of all. But so far we haven't any way to prove that they were here when Ruffles was stolen. They had gone out in the boat. Nobody saw them come back; nobody heard them."

"They could have come back while we was all working," Big said.

"And there was so much noise, we couldn't hear them," Bitsy added.

"I think that they must have carried Ruffles away in their boat," said Sandra.

"That might be why Spot lost the scent when he reached the sea," said Kirby.

"Spot's a sensible dog," Big said. "He wouldn't stop and chase his tail if the trail went on farther."

"But how can we prove anything?" Sandra asked. Nobody could think of an answer. That was the great difficulty. If only someone had seen the thieves as they carried Ruffles away.

"They may become careless," Kirby said, "and give themselves away. We must look out for that."

"Oh, dear!" Bitsy said. "I love Ruffles so much. I hope they don't hurt her."

"And we had taught the poodles all those tricks for the Concert," sighed Sandra. "Do you suppose that Leo and Pantaloon will do their tricks if Ruffles is not here?"

"Maybe we shouldn't try to have the Concert at all," Bitsy said.

"My land!" Big said. "Mr. Stonecrop, he never let *anything* interfere with the Concert."

"But we could wait a few days and have it later," Bitsy said.

Kirby had been thinking, and now he said:

"We had better have the Concert just as we had planned. The note said *after the Concert*. Whoever wrote the note must have known about the Concert, and may even expect to take a part in it."

"Besides, we shall need the Concert money to help pay the ransom," Sandra reminded them.

Late in the afternoon Mr. Locke and Mr. Black came back in their boat. They were quite sunburned and they had really caught some fish for a change.

The four children were on the beach waiting to greet them, but there was no sign of the missing poodle in their boat.

"Look!" said Mr. Locke. "Fish!"

"Them little things that swim around," said Mr. Black proudly. "This time we caught them."

"So I see," said Kirby sternly, "but where is the dog?"

"Dog?" asked Mr. Locke innocently, and Mr. Black said, "No hot dogs tonight. Tonight it's fried fish."

"I mean Ruffles," said Kirby. "What have you done with Ruffles?"

"We don't wear ruffles," Mr. Locke said; and Mr.

Black remarked: "Ruffles! That's ladies' fixings. Jimmy and me, we're tough guys. We don't have no ruffles on *us!*"

The children saw that it was useless to try to get the truth out of these rascals. There was only one thing that seemed at all like a clue. Spot walked around the two men, sniffing at their trouser legs and growling.

"Go 'way, you dog!" said Mr. Locke. "You're not the valuable kind of dog."

And Mr. Black said, "Scram!"

The two men disappeared into their cabin, and presently a sizzling sound was heard and a smell of frying fish.

"I'm sure that Spot suspects them," Kirby said.

"Spot's smarter than he looks," Big said. "I'd trust Spot's judgment a sight farther than I'd trust those men."

The children all agreed.

157

18. The Concert

Notices of the Concert at the Pink Motel had appeared in the local newspapers, and, long before the appointed time, people began to arrive. Some came in cars, some came by mule team, some people walked.

"We wouldn't miss the Concert for anything," the people said. "It is better than the moving pictures or TV. Something unusual always happens at the Pink Motel Concerts."

When the strings of electric lights were lighted, the stage looked very beautiful. Mr. Carver's stage was good and solid, and Miss Ferry's blue gauze curtains shimmered and sparkled in the artificial light as if they had threads of gold and silver woven into them. Besides the potted palms, and the green garlands, there were many gaily colored flags and flowers which had come out of Marvello's various hatboxes at a wave of his hands. Even the folding chairs from the Ladies' Uplift Society seemed glamorous in the expectant hush before the show began.

Kirby was ticket seller, and the other children were ushers. This was a busy evening for the children, because, as soon as the audience was seated, the ticket seller and the ushers would have to become performers. They would have to rush backstage and get into their costumes.

Kirby was especially busy, because somehow or other he had gotten himself into most of the acts of the show. At the same time he had not forgotten that he was the chief detective. He had asked the other children to help him keep an eye on Black and Locke. But, as a matter of fact, those two characters seemed to be behaving in a most innocent manner.

The two men appeared promptly in the costumes of pirates, ready to take part in the Concert. The only thing that seemed at all odd was that they had asked to be put on the early part of the program.

"We get real nervous if we have to wait a long time before our turn to perform," said Mr. Locke.

"If Jimmy gets nervous, he might take a nick out of my

159

ear with his knife," said Mr. Black piteously. The children could see that Mr. Black was already getting nervous.

"Besides," said Mr. Locke, "we may leave the Concert early and retire. We need our beauty sleep."

"That's right," mumbled Mr. Black. "We need our sleeping beauty."

"You must mean Cinderella," corrected Bitsy. "She was the one who had to leave on the stroke of twelve."

"The stroke of twelve?" repeated the two gangsters. It seemed to Kirby that the sound of these words made them grow paler. The two men certainly were nervous.

The tickets sold well, and Kirby was delighted to see that there would be quite a sum of money to help pay the ransom to the dognapers—that is, if it had to be paid. He still hoped that payment could be avoided. He put the money into a canvas bag, and, just before the performance began, he ran into Uncle Hiram's office and put it into the roll-top desk. He took the key and locked the desk. Then he ran back of the stage to get into his costume for the first act.

Before the show began, Mr. Mellen came onto the stage to greet the audience.

"We are happy to have you with us upon this suspicious occasion," he said. "Excuse me, I mean, this auspicious occasion. (We are all a little upset tonight because one of our performers has been kidnaped, but we shall endeavor to give you a good show anyway.) Mrs. Mellen and I welcome you. We shall probably not be here next year, as

160

we soon hope to change the unusual color of the motel and sell the place in time to go back North for our children to start school."

Here there was a long sigh of regret from the audience, and Kirby did not know whether this was at the thought of school or at the idea of changing the color of the Pink Motel. "Possibly the new owner will carry on the tradition of Hiram Stonecrop's Concert, as we are trying to do, but, if not, this will probably be the last Concert at the Pink Motel," Mr. Mellen said.

Here the sigh from the audience sounded almost like a groan, and Kirby was sorry to see that the Concert was getting off to a mournful start.

But the first act soon cheered everybody up. Kirby, in the costume of a page, wound up Uncle Hiram's old Edison phonograph with the horn shaped like a large pink morning glory. As the strains of "The Beautiful Blue Danube Waltz" floated out upon the evening air, so also did Mr. and Mrs. Brown seem to float out onto the stage. They both wore white, which set off their suntan to perfection, and they waltzed so lightly and gracefully that everyone was amazed. No one who had seen them lying on the beach day after day would have suspected them of being such delightful dancers. Sandra was proud, and everybody else was charmed. Kirby had to wind up the phonograph many times for encore after encore.

Next Jack Black and Jimmy Locke appeared in their knife-throwing act.

The four children stood beside the platform watching carefully for anything suspicious which might happen. Of course, nothing did. Mr. Locke, with his sash full of knives, was as cool as a cucumber. If Mr. Black appeared a trifle nervous, who could blame him?

"Stand up and take it, Jack," said Mr. Locke, "and don't try cutting any paper lace."

"All right, Jimmy," replied Mr. Black meekly. "I'll stand as still as I can, but please remember I only got two ears and I love each one of them."

A wooden screen had been provided as a background, and poor Mr. Black stood bravely up against this, while Mr. Locke outlined his figure in knives. The knives came so close to Jack's ears that everybody gasped. He, of course, did not dare gasp while the knives were flying. It was very exciting. In spite of himself, Kirby was obliged to admire Jimmy Locke's skill.

At the end of the knife-throwing, there was a storm of applause, and Mr. Locke stepped forward and bowed to the audience. Unfortunately Mr. Black could not come forward and bow, because one of his sleeves was pinned to the board by a knife. Tenderhearted Bitsy had to climb up on the stage and set him free by pulling out the knife.

While she was doing this, Mr. Locke held up his hand for silence, and began to make a speech. "I'm glad you're pleased," he said. "I don't know that anybody ever clapped for me before. So now I'll show you something else I can do. I'm very quick on the draw. So now I challenge any-

162

one in the audience to come up here and see if he can beat me to the draw."

There was a moment of silence when only the waves, the palms and the weather vanes could be heard. After seeing Mr. Locke's skill in throwing knives, nobody dared to come up and challenge his skill in drawing guns.

Kirby's heart began to pound. When I was a child of five, he thought, I was the quickest on the draw of any boy in the neighborhood. It's true that I am more interested in space ships now, and I'm not in very good practice—

"What?" said Mr. Locke scornfully. "Is everybody chicken?"

"Now you're talking turkey, Jimmy," said Mr. Black. "Everybody's chicken."

"*I'm* not," said Kirby. "Let me get my guns." In a moment Kirby was climbing up on the platform, fully armed and ready to face Jimmy Locke.

"It's that boy again!" said Mr. Locke. "Everywhere I turn these days, that boy is there!"

"He's got on his J. Edgar Hoover Junior G-Man badge, too," warned Mr. Black. "You better look out, Jimmy."

Mr. Carver came up on the platform now to see that everything was done fairly. First he inspected the guns to make sure that they were not loaded. He made Kirby and Mr. Locke stand back to back and then walk six paces in opposite directions.

"Now," said Mr. Carver, "turn and draw!"

Quick as a cat, Kirby turned and drew his guns. He saw with pleasure that Jimmy Locke was still struggling to get his guns out of the holster.

"Well," said Kirby modestly, "I guess I haven't lost my old speed after all."

"The winner!" cried Mr. Carver, holding up Kirby's hand. Kirby could not help thinking that this was a good omen.

"It ain't natural," said Mr. Locke crossly. "You're just a kid."

"I learned to be quick on the draw from watching television," Kirby said. "That stuff is for babies."

"*Honest?*" said Mr. Black admiringly.

"Please, Jack!" begged Mr. Locke. "That word again!"

"Excuse me, Jimmy, I always forget," sighed Mr. Black.

Quite crestfallen at their defeat, the two men took seats on the front row which was reserved for performers who had finished their part in the program.

164

"I *must* keep an eye on them," said Kirby to himself.

The Concert went very quickly after that. Bitsy and Sandra sang a duet, which was well received.

Big recited a piece, beginning, "To be or not to be," which he had learned out of Shakespeare. His mother and father and his little brothers and sisters had all been given complimentary tickets to the Concert. They sat on the next to the front row, and they were very proud of Big, as everybody else was.

Next Miss DeGree came on to do weight lifting and a drill with Indian clubs. But she was so upset about Ruffles that she began to cry in the middle of her act. She had to go and lie down while Kirby finished her performance for her.

Now Kirby quickly changed into an artist's smock and cap and assisted Miss Ferry in her chalk talk. On an easel Miss Ferry had many large sheets of brown paper. She made lightning sketches of persons in the audience. The only part she did not like to do was the eyes, because she said she needed to wear her spectacles to do eyes. So Kirby was allowed to put in the eyes, and he tried hard not to get them skew-gee. But neither Miss Ferry nor the audience seemed to mind if the eyes *were* a little skew-gee, because, after all, the greatest modern artists make them that way.

Mr. Carver came next with his Demonstration. He and Bitsy, who was wearing an oriental turban, made a pyramid of coconuts in the middle of the stage.

"Coconuts," murmured various people in the audience.

165

"What can be done with coconuts? This is certainly going to be very dull." But it took Mr. Carver only a few moments to demonstrate that even coconuts need not be dull. As Bitsy handed him the nuts, he took his new jackknife and cut here and there, very rapidly. Now he carved eyes, now a nose or a mouth.

The people in the audience, who had recently been grumbling, were now delighted to see the coconuts rapidly turned into monkeys and pirates and old gentlemen with beards. Bitsy helped with touches of red paint for lips, white for teeth and black for eyes. As the coconuts were finished, Big took over the job of handing them out to the audience. Mr. Carver always liked to give away the things he made, and the people in the folding chairs were perfectly delighted to accept his gifts.

Now came Marvello's act and, of course, Kirby assisted at this and even did a few card tricks himself. Marvello drew strings of handkerchiefs from his pocket and live white rabbits from his hat, and shot white doves into the air with an air gun. Then came the thrilling moment when he put Sandra Brown into a large cabinet, with only her head sticking out. While Mr. and Mrs. Brown and the other spectators nervously watched, Marvello took a large saw and apparently sawed Sandra in two. I shall not attempt to tell you how he did it, for I do not know. All I can say is that Sandra continued to smile, even when she seemed to be in two pieces. Presently she popped out of the cabinet, safe and sound, bowing and looking very pretty with her blond hair flying. Marvello rubbed his

166

hands in happy satisfaction. His stay at the Pink Motel had restored all of his lost skill. His act had been a success.

Last of all came the trained dog act, with all of the children and the two remaining poodles performing. They had added Spot to the act to take the place of the missing Ruffles, but Spot was a hunting dog and not a trick dog. All he could do was to sneeze and turn around after his tail. Leo and Pantaloon did their very best by jumping through hoops, and walking on their hind legs dressed in doll clothes. They played dead and said prayers. But the act was not what it would have been if Ruffles had been there to dance and walk on her front feet with her hind legs in the air. Thinking of the kidnaped poodle made everybody sad.

While the dogs were performing, Kirby suddenly remembered that he had not been keeping his eye on Black and Locke. Now, looking down into the audience, he saw that the gangsters' seats were empty. How long they had been gone he could not tell.

As soon as the act was finished, and before the applause had begun to fade, Kirby left the stage. He ran as fast as he could to Uncle Hiram's office and threw open the door. To his horror he saw that the roll-top desk was open. The lock had been broken and the bag of money taken away.

"Oh, for goodness sake!" cried Kirby, in despair. "The kidnapers have stolen the ransom money, too. *Now* what are we going to do?"

19. To Catch the Thieves

At eleven-thirty the last Concert guest departed. It was dark and quiet around the Pink Motel after the audience had gone. Kirby knew that, on the stroke of twelve, the dognapers would arrive at the old treasure chest in the palmetto grove among the gumbo limbo trees to collect the ransom and deliver the lost dog. But now that the Concert money had also disappeared, there was very little left to pay the ransom.

The regular guests of the Pink Motel gathered around the empty stage. They were still in the costumes which they had worn in the Concert, but their faces were no longer gay. Everyone was there except Jack Black and Jimmy Locke. Poor Miss DeGree was weeping again.

"What shall we do now?" the others asked.

Kirby was absent-mindedly polishing up his J. Edgar

168

Hoover Junior G-Man badge as he thought the situation over.

"We must *pretend* to put the ransom money in the chest," he said. "Big, will you bring us some newspapers, please?"

"Sure enough," Big said.

"But, if the dognapers are the ones who stole the Concert money, they'll know we do not have the ransom," objected Sandra.

"I don't think they will know for sure," Kirby said. "We might have got the money somewhere else, for all they know."

"Kirby is right," Miss Ferry said. "Anyone who tries to live by crime is sure to be very stupid or mistaken. Criminals are easily fooled."

"The time is short," Kirby said, "and this seems to be our only chance. Miss DeGree must pretend to put the money in the chest."

"Alligator's still in that chest," Big said. "Maybe we better take him out."

"No," Kirby said. "I'm counting on the alligator to help us. I think it is possible that the dognapers have never looked inside the chest. They know it is there, and they may think it is full of Uncle Hiram's treasure."

"Mr. Black and Mr. Locke saw us looking into the chest that day," said Bitsy. "Remember?"

"But they weren't close enough to see what was in it. They are very greedy. Perhaps they think that they can

169

collect the ransom money and the treasure in the old chest and everything at once and then make a speedy getaway."

"Dear me!" said Miss Ferry to herself, "if only I hadn't left the wand at home in the broom closet!"

"There is no time to lose," Kirby said. "You must all go at once and hide yourselves in the palmetto thicket among the gumbo limbo trees. Go separately and silently, as quickly as you can. Don't let anybody see you. On the stroke of twelve Miss DeGree must place the newspaper packet in the chest as if it were something very valuable."

"Is the alligator likely to nip me?" asked Miss DeGree anxiously.

"You'll have to take that chance," Kirby said. "You want to get your dog back, don't you?"

"Oh, yes, I do," Miss DeGree said, stifling a sob. "And my silver cups, too."

"If you're really afraid," Kirby said, "I'll go with you."

"Thank you," said Miss DeGree. "Please do."

"And what then, Kirby?" asked Mr. Carver.

"Well, I don't know for sure," Kirby said. "But when the villains arrive to collect the loot, I hope that we can catch them."

"How about the dogs?" asked Big.

"They might bark and give us away," said Kirby. "We must shut them up for the present. If the thieves get away, then we'll let the dogs out to help us trail them."

"Another thing worries me," said Mr. Carver. "They've

got all those knives and guns. What weapons do we have?"

"Kirby's quicker on the draw than they are," said Bitsy proudly.

"But mine are only cap guns," Kirby said.

"Marvello has his air rifle," said Sandra.

"Alas!" said Marvello, "it only shoots white doves."

"Then I suggest that everybody take a coconut," said Mr. Carver. "If properly aimed, coconuts should make a very good substitute for cannon balls. I'm sure that Hiram would have liked them used this way."

"Good!" said Kirby. "And now the important thing is secrecy and speed. Let's try not to bungle this. We must get Ruffles back safely and catch the thieves. Good luck, everybody!"

Like shadows they hurried away and hid themselves in the palmetto grove among the gumbo limbo trees. Only Kirby and Miss DeGree remained to make up the packet of false money and to await the stroke of twelve.

"Just what *is* the stroke of twelve?" asked Miss DeGree nervously. "It sounds like Cinderella's ball."

"At Miss Ferry's luncheon," Kirby said, "it was the *last* stroke of twelve. But this time I think we'd better be there for the *first* stroke. I've taken the small alarm clock out of Uncle Hiram's office. It will begin to go off promptly at twelve."

"What if we should fail?" worried Miss DeGree.

"*We can't,*" Kirby said. He said it so firmly that the sound of his own voice cheered him.

It was very dark and eerie in the swampy land behind the Pink Motel. The palmettos were as sharp and prickly as knives, and the larger trees were shrouded in ghostly moss.

At the first ring of Uncle Hiram's alarm clock Kirby and Miss DeGree walked openly to the old treasure chest and placed the packet of false ransom money in it.

The small alligator inside the chest opened his jaws, expecting to receive a frog or some pleasant bit of food from Miss Ferry. But Kirby had been smart enough not to feed him that day. The alligator was hungry. The newspaper packet did not interest him at all.

Kirby and Miss DeGree turned and went back toward the Pink Motel. When they had gone a safe distance from the chest, they hid behind trees to watch what would happen next.

For a long time nothing happened, and Kirby, who had had a long and tiring day, felt himself getting ready to yawn.

"A yawn is not as deadly as a sneeze," said Kirby to himself. It sounded like a saying of Uncle Hiram's, and Kirby determined to write it down on a piece of pink paper when he got back to the office.

Just then a twig snapped nearby. Someone was coming. There was the gleam of a flashlight among the trees. The flashlight made weird shadows among the palmetto spears and Spanish moss and gumbo limbo trees.

Two men crept quietly up to the chest.

"Now for Hiram Stonecrop's treasure, the ransom, and all the rest of it!" one of the men said.

"You think it'll be here?" asked the other man. "*Honest?*"

"Hush," said the first man crossly. "It's a hoodoo, that word is! No wonder we never bring anything off proper, and you always saying 'Honest.' "

"Well, hurry up," said the other. "This dog keeps squirming around inside my coat and nipping me. Seems like she don't consider me her friend."

"Ssh! Ssh!" said the first man. "Hold the light here while I open the chest."

"All right," the other man said. "Reach way down and be sure you get the money."

"I don't feel any Spanish gold," the first man said. "There's something kind of rough and slimy here. Hold the light closer so I can see——."

The next thing Kirby heard was an earsplitting yell. This was the signal for which Kirby had been waiting. He jumped out of hiding, shouting: "At them! Surround them! Everybody together now! Let the coconuts fly."

The others came rushing out of hiding, and for a moment the air seemed to be full of flying cannon balls.

The flashlight had fallen on the ground, but it still threw a dim light over the scene. The two dognapers were hopping about and yelling. A small alligator, with a not-unpleasant smile, was hanging onto the hand of one of them. The other seemed to be having trouble with a lively little dog which had escaped from his coat and was nipping him here and there in as many places as possible.

"Stop, thief!" cried Mr. Mellen.

"Surrender!" thundered Marvello.

"Why, forever more!" cried Mrs. Mellen, "it's those lovely gentlemen in pin-striped suits, Mr. Black and Mr. Locke. Kirby was right about them after all!"

Yes, just as everyone had suspected, Jack Black and Jimmy Locke were the dognapers. Battered by the coconuts and set upon by alligator and dog, they did not even put up a struggle to escape.

"It's no use," Mr. Locke said, when they had separated him from the alligator and given the alligator a couple of frogs to reward him for his part in the capture. "No, it's no use at all. Jack and me have tried and tried. We never succeed in bringing anything off."

"*Honest!* It's a fact," said Mr. Black.

"Don't say that word, Jack, *please!*" begged Mr. Locke.

"Let him say it," Miss Ferry said. "It's an excellent word and should be in more general use. The trouble with you is, you haven't given honesty a try."

"I have my darling Ruffles back again," said Miss De-Gree happily. "But where are my silver cups?"

"They're in a bag behind that second tree," said Mr. Locke.

"And where is the Concert money?" asked Kirby.

"But you said that was for the benefit of Humanity," said Mr. Black. "Ain't we Humanity, too?"

"If so, a person would hardly notice it," said Mr. Carver severely.

It turned out that the Concert money was safe and sound along with the silver cups.

"And Hiram's pencil," Kirby said, "that belongs in the roll-top desk."

"We're failures," Mr. Locke said sadly, taking the crooked pencil out if his pocket and restoring it to Kirby.

"I can sympathize with you, my poor fellow," the Great Marvello said. "We all have our moments of failure, but I find that by coming to the Pink Motel my powers are renewed. Possibly the Pink Motel will have a beneficial effect on you, too."

"It's made us soft, that's what!" said Mr. Locke.

"Why, ever since we come here, Jack's been losing his grip. All he really wants to do is cut lace doilies out of the pink note paper in the desk drawer. And I—I—"

"Yes?" everybody asked.

"I'm tired of crime, too. I planned that this would be my last one. I thought that, if we could locate Hiram Stonecrop's treasure, we'd be on easy street and could retire from crime."

"We thought the treasure must be in that chest," said Mr. Black. "The dognaping and taking the Concert money, that was just like soup before the main meal."

"I wonder where Hiram's treasure really is?" mused Miss Ferry. "I used to feel so sure that he had one. Now I am beginning to wonder—since none of us has found it."

20. The Seventh Weather Vane

Mr. and Mrs. Mellen, their two children, and the guests of the Pink Motel stood silent for a moment. They were all wondering, as Miss Ferry suggested, whether Hiram Stonecrop ever really had had any sort of treasure.

"It doesn't seem as if it could be money," Mr. Carver said. "Hiram never cared for money, except to give it away to people who were in need of food or clothing."

"He lived very simply," Miss Ferry said.

"Never seemed to have anything up his sleeve," observed Marvello.

"He sure enjoyed hisself," said Big.

"If he had a secret," Kirby said, "I think it must be in his roll-top desk somewhere."

"Jimmy looked there," said Mr. Black. "He never found a thing, except that funny pencil."

"And look what that did for us," sighed Jimmy Locke.

"All of those pink slips," mused Kirby. "Maybe there's something in those."

"But the pink slips," said Mr. Carver, "that's where he wrote old sayings that are so common no one heeds them any more. Hiram believed that folks should remember them more often, and look for the truth in them. That's why he wrote them down."

"You mean," wailed Mr. Locke, "that Hiram Stonecrop's treasure is only little pieces of pink paper?"

"My poor, bad man," said Miss Ferry, "don't you know that the greatest treasures in the world are things that can be written on little slips of paper or carried around in the head? Money is soon spent, or lost, or stolen by gangsters like yourself. After it is gone, what is left? Nothing! But, when you have ideas, noble thoughts, then you possess a treasure which no one can take away from you."

"There's just one thing I've thought of," Mr. Carver said. "Has anyone ever looked into the coconut marked *Hap. I?*"

"No," Kirby said. "It didn't seem important. Do you think it is?"

"Let's look," said Mr. Carver.

They all trooped back to the Pink Motel, and crowded around the door of Hiram's office. It was very late, and they were all tired. Yet no one wanted to wait until dawn to see what was in *Hap. I*. Mr. Carver went into the office and switched on the light.

"Kirby," he said, "you look."

178

So Kirby came in and took the coconut shell marked *Hap. I* off the shelf. He put his hand inside it, and he found that it contained only one very small, thin slip of pink paper. Kirby took the slip of paper out of the shell and unfolded it. He stared at it for a moment, trying to figure it out. Only two words were written on the slip of paper, and, in a puzzled voice, Kirby read them aloud:

"Try understanding"

"Well?" said everybody, "and what does that mean?" They searched each other's faces in bewilderment. But finally Mr. Carver began to smile.

"Understanding," he said. "Why, that's what old Hiram Stonecrop had. He tried to understand folks, and it was a fine way to run a motel. I always felt at home here."

"Me, too," Miss Ferry said.

"I, also," said Marvello.

"I wonder," Mr. Mellen mused, "if we could always run the Pink Motel along the same lines as Hiram did?"

"Daddy, you're going to stay!" exclaimed Kirby. And

179

Bitsy cried, "Oh, Daddy!—and keep it pink, just as it always was!"

"What do you say, my dear?" asked Mr. Mellen, turning to his wife.

"Yes, yes," said Mrs. Mellen eagerly, "to keep it pink, to try to understand each other, to be happy here and try to make everyone else happy—that really would be nice."

"If you do that, we'll all come back next year," the guests of the Pink Motel cried.

"Then it's settled," said Mr. Mellen.

As if the two words in *Hap. I* had contained some sort of magic, all of the men and women, boys and girls began shaking hands and smiling at each other. The dogs began frisking and barking. Even Mr. Black and Mr. Locke were caught up in the general friendliness and understanding, and they went about slapping the gentlemen on the back and kissing the ladies' hands.

"*Honest,* I feel real *good!*" said Mr. Black, and Mr. Locke understood so well how his friend felt that he never once thought to object to his language.

So the motel remained Pink and the Mellens stayed on. Mr. Mellen sold his office in the North, including all of his filing cabinets. For he had found that coconut shells were just as good to put things in, and much more interesting.

When school started up again, Kirby and Bitsy went to school in a pleasant country schoolhouse down by the crossroads.

180

The motel continued to grow and thrive, and soon Mr. Mellen had to build more pink cottages by the sea to accommodate all of the guests who wished to stay in this delightful place. There were many new guests, but some of the same old ones returned every year.

Miss Ferry with her hamper and Marvello with his trunk were usually the first arrivals, and they were soon followed by Mr. and Mrs. Brown and Sandra.

"This is the best place in Florida to get a suntan," Mrs. Brown would explain.

"Now, Mummy," Sandra corrected, "you know we come because we have the best time here."

"The child is right," said Mr. Brown. "Our Sandra is remarkably right, as usual."

Of course Miss P. DeGree brought her talented dogs. They had taught themselves so many tricks that she now frequently exhibited them in circuses as well as in dog shows. They were all happiest, however, when they could return to the Prancing Horse cabin at the Pink Motel.

John Black and James Locke were now busy earning an honest living, but they managed to arrange for their two-week vacation to fall at the time when their friends were at the Pink Motel. When they arrived, they brought presents for everyone, just as Mr. Carver used to do. Doubtless they got their idea from one of Hiram's pink slips, but they now understood that it is more fun to give than to take. There was always an Art Show, as well as a Concert, when they came. Miss Ferry displayed her paintings, Mr. Black displayed his pink paper lace doilies, and

Mr. Locke, who had lately taken up knitting, displayed his Argyle socks and mittens.

And what about Mr. Carver? Well, with new cottages to build, new weather vanes to whittle, and coconuts continually falling down, Mr. Carver decided to stay with the Mellens and make himself useful all the year around.

One day Kirby, Bitsy and Big stood in a proud row and watched Mr. Carver put a weather vane on top of the central cottage. Mr. Carver had studied a long time over this, but finally he had made a weather vane which seemed appropriate. Pedro, the alligator, had been allowed to go back to his swamp, but, before he was turned loose, Mr. Carver had whittled his likeness into a weather vane for Kirby's house. Above the wooden alligator, Mr. Carver also whittled out a large likeness of Kirby's J. Edgar Hoover Junior G-Man badge. The whole weather vane looked splendid, and the children approved of it. But they had never heard how it sounded. Now they stood anxiously waiting to hear what noise it would make when the wind took it.

The day was calm and sunny, and Kirby wet his finger and held it up to see if he could detect a breeze.

"In a minute," he said. "It's on its way." He was right, as usual, for in a very short time, they could hear the palm leaves beginning to rattle, as a breeze came lightly and gently in from the sea. Slowly the alligator weather vane began to turn about into the wind.

"There she blows!" said Mr. Carver happily. Then the delighted children saw that Mr. Carver had arranged it so that the wooden alligator would open and shut his jaws as he turned about in the wind.

Snap! bang! snap! the new weather vane said, and the waves roared, the palm leaves rattled, and all of the other weather vanes went *buzz, whirr, slap* and *clatter!*

The three children began to jump up and down and wave their arms and shout.

"Oh, isn't it delightful?" Bitsy shouted. And Kirby shouted back, "You bet!"

About the Author

Carol Brink has written several books for adults, but it is the children's world which claims her. She has said, "Children need the lift and thrill of imaginative writing as well as the tangible foundation of facts. It is this combination of realism and imagination which I wish very much to achieve in my own writing."

The delightful fantasies of *Baby Island*, the hilarious adventures of *The Highly Trained Dogs of Professor Petit* (a Weekly Reader Children's Book Club Selection in 1954), the historical novel, *Lad with a Whistle*, the Newbery Medal winner, *Caddie Woodlawn*, and *The Pink Motel* all testify to her success.

Books by Carol Ryrie Brink

All Over Town
Anything Can Happen on the River
Baby Island
Caddie Woodlawn
Family Grandstand
Family Sabbatical
The Highly Trained Dogs of Professor Petit
Lad with a Whistle
Mademoiselle Misfortune
Magical Melons
The Pink Motel